FURternity Leave

WHEN ALL
YOU NEED
IS FAITH

Stormy—
thank you for
your support!
de de Cox
Acts 20:35

de de Cox

Female Model:	Heaven Redmon
Male Model:	Bo Cox
Bulldog:	Candy Lacy (China Lacy / owner)
Photography and Production:	Austin Ozier / Ozier Productions
HMUA:	Scooter Minyard
Asst. to HMUA:	Jeanette Moore
Wardrobe and Design:	Andre Wilson / Style Icon Group, LLC
Location :	NULU – Louisville, KY
Inspiration :	Elizabeth Cox (FURever in our memories)
Contributor:	Robyn Thomas

Quantity sales special discounts are available on quantity purchases by corporations, associations, and others. For details, contact the publisher at the address above.

Orders by U.S. trade bookstores and wholesalers. Email info@ BeyondPublishing.net

The Beyond Publishing Speakers Bureau can bring authors to your live event. For more information or to book an event contact the Beyond Publishing Speakers Bureau speak@BeyondPublishing.net

The Author can be reached directly at BeyondPublishing.net

Manufactured and printed in the United States of America distributed globally by BeyondPublishing.net

BEYOND
PUBLISHING

New York | Los Angeles | London | Sydney

ISBN Hardcover: 978-1-637920-34-3

ISBN Softcover: 978-1-637920-35-0

DEDICATION

Psalms 36:5-7 Your love, LORD, reaches to the heavens, your faithfulness to the skies. Your righteousness is like the highest mountains, your justice like the great deep. You, LORD, preserve both people and animals.

I know that God loves our fur babies. How? Because He brought Elizabeth to our family. For the first six years of her life, she was severely neglected and abused. She was used as nothing but a breeding machine. She was kept in the dark, in a cold basement. She was never let out from the crate. She had lost several teeth from trying to gnaw her way to freedom. We received the call from the rescue (Indiana Bulldog Rescue) that she was in transport. The first question was, "Are you ready?" You bet we were!

We picked her up and immediately noticed her anxiety from being transported from one vehicle to another. Her anxiety never left her. She was not the dog who would run to the door with her leash in her mouth when you mentioned the "W" word (walk) or the "R" word (ride). She was the dog who feared leaving the inside of our home. She had more blankets and beds than our entire family put together. She was our Queen – she was Queen Elizabeth.

I say "was" because she crossed the Rainbow Bridge this year. Cancer took her from us. She was twelve young years old. On March 11, 2021, we held her and made sure she was given her favorite treat – cheese. She passed at our home with the help of Lap of Love and Dr. Kendra Healy, DVM.

For six short years, she blessed our family with her quirkiness and colic noises (always at the same time every night). We miss those noises. I don't know that we ever heard her bark. The tears and pain have not subsided. We have learned to hold them in. We brought her home. She now has a special spot on our dresser, where she will ALWAYS be safe. Cherish the minutes that become treasured moments. Elizabeth Cox – you will never be forgotten.

FURternity Leave

INTRO

What had she done? She knew it was the right thing to do in that moment. She could not turn away and just leave her in the rescue shelter. She had been through so much already. Hope needed to pull off the road and collect herself. She found a small diner and parked. She looked over at the sleeping bulldog in her front car seat. She was safe and secure. That's all Hope cared about. Hope needed to return home and begin the preparation and planning of something so fragile – life. She could not think about the "what if". That "what if" was snoring rather loudly in her car. Hope knew she had been granted a few weeks before, not only Hope's life would change, Faith's life would as well. That was the name Hope had given the momma bulldog. Faith. Isn't that what we all need – just a little faith?

CHAPTER 1

Never in Hope Sloan's life would she have imagined that she would see an act so blatant or unkind, BUT she did. After spending the weekend with her parents, Hope was enjoying the view of the landscape. She had turned the radio on and was listening to "her" kind of music. Hope was an old soul. Her mother had always referenced that saying with Hope. Belting out the words to Rick Springfield's number 1 song back in the 70s ("I Wish That I Had Jesse's Girl"), Hope noticed the truck in front of her slowing down. There was no stop sign in sight. There were no traffic lights ahead. In fact, this was the straight stretch of road that Hope loved to travel. The scenery was magnificent. The sun and clouds were just the right hue. Spring would be here shortly. Hope watched as the truck almost, but not quite, came to a stop. The door flew open, and a box was thrown from the right passenger side door. Hope could not tell if this was garbage just being pitched for no explainable reason, other than laziness. She watched as the truck sped away.

What made Hope pull over, she had no clue. It could have been curiosity, and then again, it could have been fate. Whatever it was, Hope inhaled and felt her stomach tighten with anticipation. She clenched the steering wheel. Opened the door. Walked around the front of the car and heard it. A whimpering. It was not loud, but it was a whimper. A whimper of fear or a whimper of relief, Hope did not know. The box top was open, but Hope could not see what was making the whimpering pleas inside. She knelt down on the ground and quietly pulled the corners aside.

Hope felt the tears begin to slide down her cheeks. She could not stop them. It was as if the river waters began to flow without ceasing. She wiped her face with both hands and reached in to pull the contents out. Hope knew it was an animal. She looked upwards to the heavens and prayed that the animal was okay. As she began to uncover the animal, Hope realized there was no turning back. Hope could not leave the bulldog. She was all Hope had, if she were to survive.

Hope looked down at the animal. Hope did not even think about what would happen if the animal were to bite her. She gently leaned in, and with a calming voice, she told the bulldog that all was going to be well. All was going to be fine. Hope scooped the animal up with all the strength she had and cupped her tight to her chest. The bulldog was shivering. Hope did not know if the shivering was from fear or from the cold, but she knew time was of the essence to save this fur baby. The whimpering had stopped and was replaced with uncontrollable panting. Hope placed the bulldog inside her car. *Please, oh, please, let me have extra blankets in the car.* Whenever Hope visited her parents' home, she packed a few extra necessities for a "just in case" episode. This was one of those. She popped the trunk and placed her head down in thanks. There they were. Pillows, blankets, and bottled water. She pulled the blankets out and situated them in the backseat, in order to make the bulldog feel warm. The bulldog, without hesitation, raised up to walk towards the blankets. The bulldog laid its body right smack dab in the middle of the blankets. Hope did a last-minute check on her car. She looked in the back seat one more time for good measure. Hope heard the breathing slow down and watched as the bulldog closed its eyes.

As Hope turned the ignition, she smiled. She did not know if the bulldog was a boy or a girl. She hadn't taken the time to check. Did it really matter? Would it have changed her decision? No, it didn't matter. Right now, Hope needed a veterinarian.

CHAPTER 2

As Hope was leaving Dr. True's animal rescue, she stopped. What was she doing? Hope had never fostered an animal, let alone one who was pregnant. Plus, the fact of one, who any day now, was going to give birth to four pups. When Dr. True informed Hope of how many babies the x-ray revealed, she felt as if she were going to pass out. Even Dr. True's friend, Dr. Steele sat Hope down and told her to take a breath. Oh, Hope was taking a breath. She was taking a lot of breaths. At one point, Hope felt she was going to pass out and reached for the chair. Hope then began to giggle uncontrollably. She knew that both Dr. True and Dr. Steele were concerned about Hope caring for the momma bulldog. After the initial shock of hearing several times that there were four puppies waiting to be born, Dr. True gave Hope the itemized list of steps one through ten (the do's and don't's) that Hope would need to follow regarding the momma bulldog and the birth of the babies.

Growing up, Hope had been surrounded by animals of all kinds. Living in the country, away from the hustle and bustle of the city, Hope started her early love of animals with a goldfish that her dad had won just for her at the county fair. Hope had named her goldfish, Goldie. Unfortunately, like all good goldfish, Goldie's life expectancy was not very long. Hope begged her mom and dad for another pet. This time, it was a hamster. To hear Hope's mom tell the story, all the animals that would have fit on Noah's Ark had become a part of Hope's childhood and their family. These moments became memories that Hope realized in adulthood had made her more empathetic to God's creatures.

Hope could hear the soft snoring of the momma bulldog. She had named her Faith. There was a Bible verse that came to mind: "Faith can move mountains." Hope knew that both she and Faith were going to need to move more than mountains in the next few weeks. Hope's job required at least 50 hours a week, if not more. Everything was dependent on the project that had been assigned to her and her team. Her boss was even more demanding. He was a stickler for perfection. He did not like excuses. There was always a way to make it work, and that is what required Hope's focus and commitment. She had worked her way up in the Spotlight Marketing Agency to the assistant vice president of retail accounts. Hope had a way about her. Everyone around her saw her gift. Hope knew the success was from her hard work, but it was also the fact she had a great team surrounding and supporting her. She, in return, gave them the same accolades. She knew that it was never by herself, but it was all of them together. She wished that the president/owner of Spotlight Marketing Agency, Mazdon Elliott, had seen her capabilities and willingness to go the extra hours or mile to conclude the project with perfection.

The project that had been assigned to Hope and her team before she had left to spend time with her mom and dad was the Bitty Bites Bakery. This was a new arena for the agency. Mazdon Elliott was notorious for turning down projects that related to any kind of animal. No one knew why, but all knew not to ask. Hope had heard the rumor that not only did Mr. Elliott want Bitty Bites Bakery as a client, the company needed Bitty Bites Bakery to enhance the agency's portfolio. Hope had communicated with her team that doors would be opened into the pet industry that Spotlight could never imagine.

As Hope was pulling into her driveway, her first thought was of Faith. She had rested most of the drive. Hope was going to have to communicate with her team and with Mr. Elliott the circumstances of the weekend. Hope knew her team would be ecstatic by the events. She had a feeling that Mr. Elliott would not be overly accommodating. He did not seem the type to like babies, let alone the four-legged kind.

Oh, well, she would tackle any concerns tomorrow. Right now, she and Faith needed to unpack and get ready for bed. Tomorrow was going to be a wing-dinger.

CHAPTER 3

Mazdon Elliott had deadlines to meet. As he pulled into his private parking spot, he hoped that the weekend had been beneficial to his public relations / marketing team. There were several big accounts that Spotlight Marketing Agency would be pitching this week to potential clients. Everyone needed to be on their "A" game. Mazdon had yet to be disappointed with his team. All worked together, and the efforts were noticed at the presentations to the potential clients by Mazdon.

Before he exited his car, his thoughts turned to the team and to one particular individual who kept the meeting on track. Mazdon had noticed her on several occasions. She was quiet, but she was focused. She never sat at the front of the table. She sat near the end on the right side, closest to the door. She was the first to leave the meeting. From that point, Mazdon would not see her unless another meeting was called to discuss any concerns on a campaign.

He could not fathom what had piqued his interest in her, but Mazdon had asked HR to pull her résumé.

Her name was Hope Sloan. She had been with the agency for two years. She had moved up the ladder in the agency, without too much fanfare. She was the assistant vice president of retail accounts. This title was nothing to sneeze at and yet, Mazdon had never heard her boast or brag about the title or herself. He knew that she did not have family in town. He had overheard several members of her team speaking regarding weekend plans. He knew she would be going out of town to visit her mother and father. Her personal address was on the outskirts of town. She had listed only two positions under employment history. These companies were insignificant. They were not the size of Spotlight Marketing Agency, but still reputable.

Mazdon thought to himself, *I know most of the team except for her. Well, today that is about to change. I will request a one-on-one meeting with Miss Hope Sloan.* Mazdon felt good about the decision. He knew that Spotlight needed to venture into new arenas. Today's meeting with Bitty Bites Bakery would be the catalyst to open the door for new endeavors and even bigger adventures.

Mazdon walked with deliberate steps into the building and took the elevator to the floor of the agency. The entire 10th floor belonged to the agency. As soon as you stepped off the elevator, you felt the vibrance. The interior was bright with all the colors of the sun (from the rising to the setting). Mazdon had never prohibited his employees from adding that "extra touch" to their offices. He actually encouraged it. Statistics showed that making the work environment closer to the ambience of home, the less employees would miss work days. At first, Mazdon had thought his father was a bit off his game by keeping statistics such as this, but in the long run, his father was correct. There was not one desk that did not hold pictures of their family, wedding pictures, baby pictures, and in some cases, pictures of their pets.

Mazdon was an only child. He had never been married, and according to the tabloids, "no love interest had been found or located." Mazdon had been declared one of the most eligible bachelors in the city. If Mazdon were honest and cared enough to keep the public informed, he would tell them he did not have time for a girlfriend, wife, children, nor even pets. His time was consumed with the continuation of a legacy. The agency. Mazdon could remember many days playing or taking a nap underneath his father's big, cherry, wooden desk. Mazdon's mother had passed several days after his birth from complications. His father did not like to talk about Mazdon's mother. There were very few pictures in the home. Mazdon realized at a tender age that his father kept his feelings to himself regarding his mother. Mazdon's father was not mean, but he did display emotion when Mazdon had done what was asked or required of him. His father would never state the words "well done", but only give a nod in Mazdon's direction to let him know he was well aware of Mazdon's accomplishments. The elevator stopped, and the doors opened.

Mazdon greeted Andee, the main receptionist, with a hello and asked if the conference room was clean and ready for the morning meeting. She nodded with a smile and stated all was ready. Coffee, water, juice, donuts, muffins and bagels – it was going to be a sugar high Monday. At least, all would be wired after the conclusion of the meeting and ready to hit the ground running. Mazdon smiled to himself. He loved Mondays. Mondays were not to be feared. They were the beginning of something new. His father had taught him that saying. Mazdon could hear his father reiterating this simple sentence every Monday morning that Mazdon was running late for school. Those Monday mornings were just a bear, but they were also memories that Mazdon cherished of his father's wit and humor.

The knock on Mazdon's office door brought him back to the future. He announced "come in". Andee smiled and informed him that all had arrived for

Monday's meeting. Mazdon did not need to ask if pen, notepad, and computer were placed on the table in preparation for the meeting. Andee was efficient and had the routine down pat. Mazdon thanked her. He stood up. Today was the dry run of the ad campaign that would be pitched later in the afternoon to Bitty Bites Bakery. Mazdon stood and turned. Mondays were not to be feared.

CHAPTER 4

Hope had set the alarm an hour prior to her normal routine. She feared that from this day forward, there would never be normal again. Not only was her life about to be flipped upside down, but so was Faith's. Hope was nervous. Faith had slept in her bed all night. Hope remembered what Dr. True had told her. She is in unfamiliar surroundings and may be a bit timid. Take time to introduce her to your home. And most important, just show her love.

Hope woke up. She remembered setting the alarm. Why had it not gone off? She reached to check the time. It was 9:00 a.m. Oh my gosh. She blinked and realized that the alarm was set for p.m. and not a.m. Hope was late. Hope had never been late. This was her pet peeve of any meeting. Arrive at least 10 to 15 minutes early. That way, she could get the seat nearest to the door and furthest from him. There was no chance of that. The meeting had been scheduled for 10:00 a.m. to give everyone time to go through emails and begin the preparation for the campaign meetings scheduled for the day. Hope would not have time to shower. She needed to walk Faith, feed her, get dressed, and race like a banshee to get to the meeting. Easier said than done. Hope looked over at Faith, who was sleeping—and even snoring—without a care in the world. Hope reached for the harness to place on Faith, thinking she would get up. Nope. No movement. One eye opened and stared at Faith with a statement of "not today". Hope gently placed the harness on Faith and tried to get her to stand up. Nothing. There was no way that Faith did not have to go outside and do her business. Hope did the only thing she could. She picked Faith up. There was no time to waste. In her PJs, carrying a bulldog, Hope walked outside and popped Faith on the grass. "Please, girl, I need you to go potty." Hope watched as Faith squatted and then turned to look at Hope to see the assurance that she had done well. Hope laughed. "Yes, I will get you a treat." Hope turned, and just like it had been a normal routine, Faith followed her back into the house. Hope walked to the cupboard, where Faith's food had been stored, and poured out one cup. Dr. True had given strict instructions: one cup in the morning and one cup in the evening.

Hope knew she had about ten minutes to gather her wits about her and get ready for work. There was no time to shower. She washed her face and brushed her teeth. She rolled her deodorant on and threw on a dress that she could wear with her riding boots. Hope was ready. The question was: was she prepared? Several scenarios kept playing over in her mind. Sneaking in and not being seen. Tardiness was not one of Hope's traits. She made every attempt to be early to meetings, especially those related to a campaign. Preparation was key to everything. In life, in work, in goals, and especially, in your dreams. Hope knew, without a doubt, the meeting with Bitty Bites Bakery would change the course of her career.

She made sure Faith had water in her crate and coaxed her in with a treat. Hope had purchased the largest crate possible for Faith. Shoot, Hope could even stand up inside of the crate. Hope needed to come home at lunch to check on Faith. She did not want her to be stuck in the crate all day.

And then, the emotions hit. Hope wanted to sit down and cry. She had not really thought about how "fostering" an animal was going to change her daily routine. This morning had demonstrated to Hope that upon her return home, she needed a plan. The thought of leaving Faith *all* day with no one to tend to her needs was more than Hope could bear. What if she got thirsty? What if she ate all her food and was still hungry? What if she needed to go to potty? Hope wanted to just pack

Faith up and take her to work with her. Hope knew that was not an option. Hope leaned down one last time, and reached inside to pet Faith as assurance. Faith lifted her paw, as if to say goodbye. Well, that's all it took for Hope to realize that Faith was stuck with her.

Hope opened the front door, grabbed her briefcase, and did a double check on the file. She took one last look at Faith, who had begun to snore again. *Lawd, how did she not wake herself up?* Hope beeped the car door open. Seatbelt locked. Hope knew if anyone were going to be mean or cross today, she would break down in tears. She was a hot mess. She knew it, and probably everyone else in the agency would know by the time she arrived. Hope looked in the rearview mirror. This was as good as it was going to get. Hope was ready to tackle anyone and everything.

CHAPTER 5

Mazdon had walked into the conference room. He did a cordial good morning to the team and watched as they began to take their seats in preparation for the trial pitch to Bitty Bites Bakery. Mazdon smiled to himself. Humans were all creatures of habit and routine. Pens, notepads, and computers were placed on the table, with bottled water and coffee in the middle. An itinerary had been placed in each seat for the team. Karey, Lacie, Clay, Michael, Hailey, and Hope – this was the team. Mazdon stopped. The team, the number of bodies in the room, was not accurate. Mazdon felt it. She was *not* there. The rest of the team was incomplete. Where was she? What was going on? This was a very important meeting; did she not realize this? What could take precedence over this?

Mazdon walked to the head of the table and pulled the chair out. He cleared his throat, and all the heads in the room turned to him. Each knew the "clearing of the throat" was the signal that Mazdon was ready to begin the day and the agenda. It was as if a light went off at the same time with everyone. First, Karey asked the question, "Where is she?", and then, the others began to shake their heads while whispering, "I don't know." Mazdon had heard enough. He looked at the team and asked, "Does anyone know where she is—and by she, I mean Hope Sloan?"

One by one, they each said, "I don't know." It was now ten minutes after the hour. Mazdon hated tardiness. Either you were able to attend or not. If you were not, then he expected some type of notification, such as an email or telephone call. Neither of those had taken place this morning.

"Has anyone attempted to call Ms. Sloan and find out what the delay seems to be?" All nodded no. "Okay, then, does anyone have her number, and I will make the call to determine her whereabouts?" Hailey looked at the team. If she saw Mr. Elliott's number come across her cell, she definitely would *not* answer it. Hailey was prayerful that Hope would recognize his number and not answer.

Hope was parking her car. The phone, for the last ten minutes, had been ringing incessantly. She did not recognize the number. Hope never answered a number she did not recognize. More than likely, it was a robo call or one of those car warranty expiration reminders. Hope did not have time for either. She took her cell out of purse. Again, the same number. She would give them credit for being persistent. Hope was going to put a stop to this right here and now. Hope hit the green button and started with, "No, I don't have a car, I drive a horse and buggy. No, I don't need any hotel rewards or points. And I definitely do not need Medicare or Social Security benefits; I'm just 25 years old." She was just about ready to disconnect, when she heard a male voice laughing.

Before she could disconnect the conversation, Hope recognized the voice. It was her boss. It was Mazdon Elliott. The next words made Hope's heart skip a beat. She then heard, "Ms. Sloan, it's Mr. Elliott. We have been waiting to get the meeting started regarding Bitty Bites Bakery campaign pitch. Unfortunately, someone is missing. Any guesses who that might be?" Hope could hear the impatience in that sarcastic hint. "I need you here in the conference room with us. I am going to assume there is an explanation as to why your presence is not here at this moment." Hope didn't know if she should tell him the truth or just agree and answer his question. She decided the latter would be the best choice. "Mr. Elliott, I apologize. There were unexpected issues that took place at my home this morning that could not be avoided. I am in the parking lot and walking in. I'll be there in less than ten minutes."

CHAPTER 6

Was he dialing the right number? Did this woman never answer her calls? Was she driving and could not answer her cell? Or was she just choosing not to pay attention to her cell ringing? The more he attempted, the more frustrated he became with the fact that he was being ignored. Finally, his call was picked up. He did not even hear a "hello". The voice aggressively started with, "No." Mazdon listened to the end of her conversation and then busted out laughing. He couldn't help himself. No one had told him "no", and no one had ever told him that they drove a horse and buggy for transportation, especially in the year 2021. He listened to Hope Sloan, all the way to the end. He was especially intrigued with the fact that she was "just 25 years old."

Ten minutes she had stated. She had about ten more seconds, and then, he would need to start the meeting, and, to prove a point (not just to Hope Sloan, but to all in attendance), the conference room doors would be locked, and the meeting would begin with or without her.

Mazdon could feel the stares. He knew the entire room was wondering why he was laughing. Mazdon slowly turned around to begin the explanation that he knew all were waiting to hear. Out of the corner of his eye, he spotted Hope Sloan. She looked a bit panicked. He moved towards the door and opened it, so she would not have to encounter any more distractions. Hope was doing her best imitation of a sprinter in the 100-yard dash while trying to maintain a bit of composure before she entered the meeting. Too late. He saw her. He was holding the door. She could not look at him. She thanked Mr. Elliott for holding the door. Mazdon could tell that Hope had every intention of taking her seat at the back of the table, just as she had done so many times before. But not today. He wanted to hear what her ideas were on the campaign and how to better entice Bitty Bites Bakery to hire the agency. Hope did not make it to "her" seat, because Mazdon gently touched her elbow and guided Hope to the very front seat. "I cannot wait to hear your input this morning, Ms. Sloan. Are we ready, or is there another matter that requires your attention?" Hope could tell he was not in the best of moods. Sarcasm and facetiousness were dripping from both corners of his lips. "No sir, I'm ready." Hope looked at her team. Not a word was uttered. All nodded in agreement. "Good, we don't have time to waste. Let's see what you have."

Hope came to the end of the presentation and the video. She looked at Michael and asked if the lights could be turned back on. This was it. He either hated it or liked it. He never made any comments during the pitch. He made notes. Hope knew, because she heard his pen. She did not know if you could really hear a "pen", but she sure heard the clicking and then the pen being placed down on the notepad. Oh yeah, he had made notes.

Mazdon stood up. He picked his notepad up. He knew they were expecting the worst and, actually, he had been expecting the worst as well, *but* the presentation was incredible. All points of concern had been brought to the forefront of the video. The video was not over-the-top. It focused on the relationship that the bakery had, not just with the animals, but with the pet owners. Mazdon knew that most folk, who had grown up with pets, would continue their love for animals into adulthood and into their senior years. He was pleasantly surprised. He did want to go over a few small details. Overall, the team had done it. Bitty Bites Bakery could not say no. He smiled, and Mazdon could see the team's shoulders relax. "Guys, I am pleased, and I know the client will be pleased. Great job. I just want to discuss a few minor details with Ms. Sloan. We will meet later in the week to discuss the next project. Again, thank you."

Hope did not hear "thank you". The words that kept resonating in her mind were "I just want to discuss". What did he want to discuss? How long would the discussion be? Why was she the only one remaining in the conference room? Hope could not help herself. She began to wring her hands together. She had never been left alone with her boss. The opportunity never presented itself, because she always was at the end of the table, near the exit. Not today. There was no exit. She was stuck.

Hope watched as her friends left, each one turning around to give her the thumbs up. Hope smiled in acknowledgement. She waited until she could wait no longer. "Was everything okay? Is there anything that needs to be changed?" Mazdon turned towards her. "No, all is good. I am pleased with the presentation. To be honest, you seem a bit out of sorts. Is there a reason why you were late to the presentation?" Hope could not believe she was having a conversation with Mazdon. During her employment at the agency, she had *never* had to nor asked to speak to him. And now, the conference room seemed really small, and he appeared larger than life, and she was going to pass out. It could have been all that had taken place within the last 72 hours, but the room was spinning. She fixed her eyes on Mazdon. "No sir. Nothing is wrong. I set the alarm for the incorrect time. Trust me, I am always on time. I apologize for today. It will not happen again." She reached for the handle on the conference room door and was like the mist in the wind – gone in silence.

She left. Did he even get a word in edgewise? Did he say what needed to be said? Did she just give him the brush off? What just happened? There was no discussion. Heck, there was not even an acknowledgement to continue the discussion. Mazdon retrieved his iPad and notes taken. Right now, he needed to prepare for the afternoon presentation with the Bitty Bites Bakery. Later, he would address his concerns with Hope.

CHAPTER 7

Hope entered her office and closed the door. She leaned back against the door. She inhaled slowly. In and out. Lawd, what had she done? She did not offer nor give him time to ask any further questions. She reached for her desk and moved around for support. As she sat down, there was a knock at the door. The door slowly opened, and Lacie poked her head in.

"Can I come in?"

Hope laughed. "Well, yes, of course." Lacie sat down in the chair across from Hope's desk. She rubbed her hand across her head and then her lips.

"Hope, is there anything you want to tell me? You are NEVER late. And that is to anything. Spill it," Lacie told her as a matter of fact.

Hope fell forward on to her desk and placed her head on her arms. "Lacie, I think I have bitten off more than I can chew. I am going to be preparing for the birth of babies..." All Lacie could focus on was the word "babies".

"What do you mean babies? Who is having babies? Are you fostering? Did you adopt? How did this happen?"

Hope loved Lacie. Their relationship was more like big sister, little sister. There was only a year that separated them in age. Upon arrival to the agency, Lacie had trained Hope. Both had moved up the ladder of success together at the agency. Each offered a specific area of expertise and knowledge. Hope and Lacie had also agreed to cross-train at their jobs. Wasn't there an old saying "that when one or more are gathered, there is strength in numbers", Hope had commented to Lacie. Why not take this opportunity and be more knowledgeable about the industry? Hope had been promoted before Lacie, and yet, there was no animosity about Hope being Lacie's supervisor. Hope explained to Lacie that it was only a comma that was at the end of Hope's name with the title. The title and promotion were great, but at the end of the day, the comma disappeared. When the day was over, she was Hope, Lacie's best friend. This entire statement is what made their friendship strong. Lacie loved how Hope use the analogy of the comma with her title.

Lacie did not have time to ask at the morning meeting why Hope was late. She knew there was more to the story than the excuse Hope supplied. Lacie leaned across the desk. Hope's eyes were red, as if she had been crying or rubbing them. "Hey, you ready to tell me what is really going on? I am not here to judge you. You know this. But you are seriously off your A game. You mentioned the word babies."

Hope looked up. She smiled. Lacie was her confidante. Hope knew that whatever was spoken behind the closed doors would remain behind closed doors. "Yes, you heard the word babies. But it's not what you think. Trust me," Hope stated.

Lacie shook her head. "Okay. Now I am really concerned. The plural of baby is babies, correct? You mentioned the plural. Like, as in more than one," Lacie told her. They both looked at each and burst into laughter. Lacie began the next sentence with a giggle. "Can you tell me how this happened?"

Hope knew her friend was trying to muddle through the darkness that she had left her in this morning. "Well, I found her on the side of the road. I watched as she was thrown from the vehicle. I stopped and picked her up. I knew that she needed to see a doctor. I drove to the nearest ER. It was confirmed. There are four."

Lacie jumped up. "Who was thrown? Four what? What are you involved in? Is it legal? You know you can tell me anything. I will not judge you, pinky swear," Lacie kept repeating over and over.

Hope pushed herself away from her desk, stood up, and walked over and hugged Lacie. "It's going to be okay, Lacie. It has to be okay."

Lacie looked at her and squeezed both Hope's hands. "One more time, please with the explanation. I promise I'm listening now," Lacie told her.

And so, Hope began the story of how while driving home, she had witnessed a box being thrown from a truck. Hope had pulled over, because her gut instinct told her there was something inside that box. She stopped, looked in the box, and there she was. A bulldog. Hope found the nearest vet, which happened to be a rescue shelter, too. The doctor did an examination of the bulldog and told Hope that the little momma would be giving birth in the next few weeks to several babies. Hope could not leave her at the facility. So instead, Hope brought her home. And that is the real reason why she was late this morning. "And, there you go. The truth, plain and simple," Hope stated, without blinking an eye. "I couldn't leave her, Lacie. I was all she had."

Lacie nodded. "You do realize the responsibility that you have just undertaken. Not just one, but add four more, and you have five huge responsibilities."

Hope laughed. "I know. It's a huge commitment on my part. Not just when the puppies are born, but to make sure they are healthy and safe and then to find homes. Oh, I have a checklist of the dos and don'ts with the breed. Right now, the goal is to find a vet here in town who knows the breed and the complications that arise with giving birth. Bulldogs typically must have a C-section. I cannot lose her, Lacie."

Lacie nodded, and stated, "Then there is no time to waste. Not only do we have to tweak a few things with the Bitty Bites Bakery campaign, we need to find a vet as soon as possible. So, let's get to it. I am here to help. Just tell me the first item on our agenda."

For the rest of the morning and into the middle part of the afternoon, Hope and Lacie made calls to the top five vets listed in the city. Hope and Lacie had made a list of questions to ask. The checklist was completed, and they huddled for comparisons. A decision was made that Dr. Jedidiah Bayley of Pawsabilities Animal Hospital would be Faith's vet. An appointment was scheduled for Friday for introductions. While there, Dr. Bayley would do an x-ray to confirm the number of puppies Faith was carrying. A scheduled C-section would take place when it was time for the puppies to be born. All had been set in motion. Now, to tackle the revisions of the Bitty Bites Bakery campaign.

The Bitty Bites Bakery owner and the director of public relations and marketing would be arriving at 3:00 p.m. for the presentation and to sign the contract. Hope instilled the team with some words of wisdom: never to hope for the win, but to plan for the win. As she and Lacie sat down to review the branding concept and to generate the last few video slides, Hope knew they had gone the extra mile. The "B" would be used as a triple threat concept for the bakery. There would be one to two commercials produced. Hope had stayed under budget. It was close, but she had kept the promise about dollars allotted to both Bitty Bites Bakery and Mazdon. Lacie sighed and gave Hope the thumbs up.

"It's ingenious," Lacie stated.

Hope nodded, "It sure is."

CHAPTER 8

Mazdon had shut the door to his office. He had instructed his assistant, Maya, that he was not to be disturbed until fifteen minutes before the meeting. Mazdon stood at his office window. Why was this woman stealing his thoughts? Who was Hope Sloan? And why was he allowing his concentration to be placed on her? Mazdon shook his head. Today was the first time he had paid attention to her. There was no way around seeing her, since she had arrived late to the meeting. From his recollection, this was the first time in Hope Sloan's employment with the agency that she had been late. Something was out of the ordinary. He couldn't put his finger on the problem, but there was something not right. This woman had intrigued him. Was it because he couldn't get a word in edgewise? She had dismissed him as if were invisible. Why was she late today? Why all of a sudden? Mazdon placed the call to human resources and requested the employment file on Hope Sloan. He wanted to view her file. The biggest question that kept bothering Mazdon was how long had Hope been with the agency and why had he never noticed her.

The file referencing Hope Sloan was brought to Mazdon within the hour. He rarely took lunch, because meetings and deadlines typically interfered. Today was no exception. He sat down at his desk and laid open the file. Hope Sloan had been with the agency going on three years. He immediately saw where she had been promoted early on in her career with the agency. She had never used any vacation days. She had only taken one sick day. She was the epitome of what every boss desired – she never took time away from the company. She was a workaholic or she didn't have a life. Mazdon was curious. More curious than he had been this morning. The clients were due to arrive in fifteen minutes. Mazdon gathered his notes and computer. He walked down the hallway and cleared his throat. Most of the team knew that was the "signal". All should be picking up their materials and any displays that would be presented to the client. Preparation was key to any endeavor. Mazdon walked in the conference room. He did a quick perusal of the room. Everything looked as it should. Karey and Hailey were checking the computer and cords. Clay and Lacie were displaying the boards and materials around the table for each individual who would be sitting in on the presentation. Michael was checking the television screen and …. where was she? She was the one who always made the presentation to the client. Yet, she was not here.

"Lacie, please tell me that Hope is NOT going to be late again." Mazdon knew Lacie realized he was not just concerned, but was becoming upset.

"No, she should be here any moment. I'll just run down the hall to see what's taking so long," Lacie stated.

"Actually, I'll check on Ms. Sloan," Mazdon replied. Mazdon reached for the handle of the door when the other side opened to reveal Ms. Sloan. "Glad you could join us, Ms. Sloan. We are ready for the Bitty Bites Bakery, correct?" Mazdon inquired.

Hope knew she was wasting time. There was no way around her dilemma. There was no way around the fact that she was not ready to be a fur baby momma. She was out of her league. The more she thought about Faith, the more she knew she was going to need help and the biggest thing of all: time. Time off to take care of Faith and the puppies. "Yes, Mr. Elliott. All is ready. There is nothing to worry about." What a lie that was. Hope's stomach was in knots. It was not just doing flips; it was doing back handsprings. Hope winked at the team. She walked to the front of the room. Hope took a deep breath. She prayed that all involved would be as impressed as she was and that the meeting was short, sweet, and to the point.

The conference room phone ringing startled Hope back to the present. She heard Mazdon acknowledge to the receptionist, Andee, of the fact that all were in the reception area and to send the president/ owner of Bitty Bites Bakery in the direction of the conference room. The plan was always the same. Mazdon would meet them as they were coming down the hallway and lead them into the conference room, where he knew the team was waiting. He would handle the introductions. Even though there were no assignment of seats, all knew it was like going to church. Everyone knew where Granny sat *every* Sunday, and if someone were in her pew, eyebrows were raised, and the "whispering" began. Hope smiled. Let's get the show on the road.

CHAPTER 9

The meeting was a success. Bitty Bites Bakery had signed. Not just the draft of the campaign, but the contract to continue the association with Spotlight Marketing Agency. Hands were shaken. Deadlines for the first billboard display and commercial play were agreed upon. *Yes,* Mazdon thought to himself, *today is the first day of many days with Bitty Bites Bakery.* Statistics showed that when the initial contact was made to sign the client, the follow up was key to retain the client for years to come. This was the make-it-or-break-it rule in the ad industry. Mazdon knew that after today's contract signing, Bitty Bites Bakery would be this client.

He had escorted the president and vice president of the bakery towards the elevator. Mazdon thanked them for their time today and informed them someone from the team would email all that had been discussed and future dates to mark. As Mazdon was preparing to enter the conference room, he could hear their voices. From just the tone of the words that could be heard, Mazdon knew they were excited with the outcome of the meeting.

He opened the conference room door. All eyes turned towards Mazdon. Lacie, Clay, Michael, and Hailey walked toward Mazdon and offered their congratulations and left to return to their offices. Mazdon smiled in acknowledgement and thanked each one. As Mazdon left, he turned back to survey the room. Someone was missing. She was not there. Mazdon could not help but wonder where she disappeared to so quickly. Why had she not remained with the others? What was so important that she could not remain with the team? Mazdon opened the conference room door. He knew the direction he was headed.

Lacie heard those footsteps coming down the hallway. They were heavy and determined. Lacie knew she was not there. As the meeting had come to a conclusion, Hope had touched Lacie's arm to get her attention. "I need to return home. If anything comes up, you know how to reach me," Hope told Lacie. Lacie watched as the elevator doors closed with Hope inside. She walked back down the hallway. Lacie closed her office doors and opened the note that Hope had given her. Lacie read the note.

"To make the story short, because I know you hate reading long excuses, this morning, I had to get Faith situated for the morning. You know the drill.

Potty, water, food, and coaxing into a crate. I was a bit frazzled, because I did not realize the amount of time that I needed to spend with Faith. And before you say it, I know I have bit off more than I can chew."

Before she could make a call to Hope to inform her that she would take care of any issues for the remainder of the business day, there was a knock at the door. She knew by the knock it was Mazdon. Lacie also knew he would not ask anyone else but her about Hope's whereabouts. The question was whether Lacie should tell him. Lacie stood up. Opened the door. She could tell he was going to ask.

Mazdon did not need or want to waste time. He knew that Hope and Lacie were the best of friends. He just needed an answer to *one* question: what was going on with Hope Sloan?

Lacie opened her office door. Mazdon asked if they could speak for a few moments about this morning and the Bitty Bites Bakery campaign.

"Of course," Lacie calmly stated.

Mazdon did not wait to skirt the elephant in the room. He immediately asked, "Is there anything you want to divulge about Ms. Sloan and her frazzled appearance this morning at the meeting?"

Lacie started with the easiest answer first. "I don't think she was frazzled, just a bit in a hurry. The pitch was successful. Bitty Bites Bakery is now a client."

Mazdon laughed. "Going to go down with the ship, are you? Okay. Just let her know I need to see her to finalize a few concerns that Bitty Bites noted. I would like to have it completed before the end of the day."

Lacie did the only thing she could do. She nodded her head. Mazdon thanked her for conveying the message, turned, and left. Lacie closed the door, leaned back, and took a deep breath. Dealing with a potential client and pitching a campaign was ten times better than having to do a one-on-one face-to-face with the boss. Lawd, did Hope owe her.

The elevator was taking forever to get to the first floor. Hope did not know why, but she felt very uneasy about Faith and leaving her this morning. The doors opened, and Hope walked briskly to the parking lot. As she was driving home, Hope could only think about what if Faith had gone in to premature labor. There was always that possibility.

Hope forgot about the speed bump leading into her subdivision. She flew over it like she was Bo and Luke on *The Dukes of Hazzard*. The car came down with a thud. She knew she was not the only one who had been airborne or whose vehicle may lose its car doors because of the hit back to the pavement.

She pulled into the driveway. The car felt restricted. Hope jerked the car into park and jumped out. She almost fell out of her car. She began to laugh hysterically. She could not control the emotions that had overcome her. She encountered problems with the key fitting in the lock. *Really, what else could delay getting inside?* As she pushed the door open, she heard a noise that could wake the dead. She walked into the kitchen where she had left Faith in the crate.

Faith was sleeping like a baby, with her tongue sticking out. As for the noise, that was Faith, too. Hope began to cry. She had no idea why. She bent down to look at Faith. One eye was open. One eye was closed.

"I know you see me, silly girl. If you only knew how worried I was about you." Hope unlocked the crate. The crate was large enough for Hope to climb in. And that's what she did. She began to talk to Faith about her day. Hope knew that Faith enjoyed having her back legs and toes massaged. Hope started with the opener with Faith, "Do you want the good news first or the bad news first? Let's start with the good news. The agency is now handling Bitty Bites Bakery campaign. They signed. The bad news. My boss is getting nosy about my tardiness and my focus. Eventually, I'm going to have to tell him I need time off to take care of you." Hope inhaled. Faith raised up and nudged her head into Hope's hands. "I know, you're hungry. Let's see what's cooking. And for good measure, let's go potty."

Hope was frozen. What was she doing? Could she do this? She looked outside in the backyard, where Faith was trying to locate "just" the right spot to do her business. Afterwards, Faith kicked both her back legs, as if she were a bull getting ready to charge. Hope watched as Faith waddled back to the deck. Faith's little belly was almost, but not quite, rubbing the grass. Friday's appointment with Dr. Bayley could not arrive fast enough. Hope had told HR that she needed the entire day off. Hope shook her head. HR told her that she had accumulated six weeks of PTO (paid time off). Hope knew she had banked weeks, but she had no idea it was this much. These days were going to come in handy.

Hope sat down at the table with pen and pad and began "the to do list". She could hear Faith. She was not just eating; Faith was woofing down her food. There were several "hot" topics that required attention. The vet appointment and the date that Faith would delivery was priority. Hope had the "come to JESUS" meeting with Dr. True. She had informed Hope that most female bulldogs necessitated a C-section. This was the safest way for both momma and the puppies. Hope would need to take a room and rearrange it to make it accommodating. There would be three areas: 1) for Faith to rest; 2) for the puppies to be kept while sleeping; and 3) for Faith to nurse. Then, there was the extra nourishment for the puppies, which required formula and syringe. A few stuffed animals would be positioned where the puppies would sleep, to entice them to explore and climb, building strong muscles. Hope shook her head. Was this what motherhood consisted of – panic and lists? Dr. Bayley would do an ultrasound on Friday. Hope knew there was more than one. She just prayed there were not more than three.

Hope felt Faith's breath against her foot. She reached down to pet her. Faith tilted her head, so Hope could have access to that one special spot – her chin. Hope felt a small tear begin. There was no time to cry. There was no one but Hope and Faith.

CHAPTER 10

Hope heard the cell phone buzz. Lacie had texted Hope about Mazdon's concerns. She added that she would be over after work to fill Hope in on the remainder of the afternoon. What concerns? What else needed to be "filled in"? Hope was confident that all concerns had been addressed and that the client, Bitty Bites Bakery, was more than satisfied with all that Spotlight Marketing Agency had presented and agreed to. In Hope's mind, there was nothing left to discuss or change. Evidently, she was mistaken. Well, the only thing that Hope could do was wait. Patience was not Hope's strong suit. She did not want to call Lacie, just in case someone walked in on their conversation. That someone being, Mazdon. Hope could not put her finger on it, but she was not liking the tone of the text or that word "concerns". No matter, Hope would wait.

Lacie knew Hope was pondering what could have gone wrong, when in actuality, nothing had gone wrong. Bitty Bites Bakery had requested new timeframes and deadlines on the branding debut. Lacie knew the deadlines could be met. She felt confident that after speaking with Hope tonight, Mazdon would feel encouraged with all revisions.

Leaving the office, Lacie did not want to be cornered by Mazdon. She had received the text from Hope. She knew that Hope was more concerned than she let on. Lacie also knew that Hope felt she had bit off more than she could chew. Faith was a huge time commitment, and then to add on the birth of the puppies, was another event for Hope's anxiety to make an appearance. Lacie needed to make a quick getaway without being noticed. She had made it to the elevator and pushed the down button. Lacie did not have time to wait. She turned to head towards the stairs. It was too late. He was standing in her path. Lacie could only think that her best friend, Hope, who was at home with her dog, Faith, was going to owe her big time. And Lacie was not afraid to tell her this fact.

"Mazdon," Lacie began. "Is there anything that needs to be completed before leaving? The team and I reviewed all the documentation and changes. Everything looks good for Bitty Bites Bakery to return tomorrow and sign the revised agreement. I'll see you in the morning."

Mazdon couldn't help but smile. He realized what Lacie was trying to accomplish. To leave without speaking to him. "Lacie, I need to know she will be here, no matter what. There are just a few more things I'll need Hope's help with."

Lacie nodded. "I'm sure she will be. I'll follow up with her tonight when I arrive at my home."

Mazdon nodded. The elevator doors opened. He placed in his hand inside the opening, so the elevator eyes would sense his presence and remain open. "Here you go, Lacie. See you bright and early tomorrow."

Lacie texted Hope from her car. "Be ready for tomorrow. Changes need to be made. He wants you in the office. You have to be here." Hope did not want any company, not even Lacie. She texted Lacie and explained that she was preparing for the vet appointment in the morning and that if anything came up out of the ordinary, Lacie knew where to find her. Hope prepared Faith for the evening. She was ready for bed. Tomorrow was a big day for everyone.

Hope could not sleep. Had she gone to bed too early? Lawd, she was turning into her parents. Up at the crack of dawn with the chickens and in the bed before 7 o'clock p.m. Hope used to tease her parents about turning in too early. Something was not right. She did not hear Faith snoring. Since bringing Faith home, snoring was the dead giveaway that all was well for the evening. Hope leaned up on her elbow. Nope, there was no noise from Faith. This was not the norm. Hope flung the covers back and jumped out of bed.

When she entered the kitchen, her heart skipped a beat. Faith was laying on her side with her tongue hanging out. She was not panting. Her breathing was slow. Hope did not waste time. She called Dr. Bayley who they would be seeing later today. Of course, it was early morning, and it went to the answering service. Hope told the service of the emergency. The service was placing the call to Dr. Bayley. They advised Hope to go ahead and prepare to bring Faith in. Hope told them she would be at Dr. Bayley's office in less than thirty minutes.

She hung the telephone up and sat down on the floor, rubbing Faith to calm her down. "It's going to be okay. I promise." Hope kissed Faith on the nose and started the packing process. There was no time to shower or even brush her teeth. Hope threw on her sweatshirt and sweatpants. She did not care that she didn't even put her bra and panties on. These items were not a priority. Hope gathered several blankets and opened the front door. She started her vehicle and turned the heat on to warm it up. It was still a bit chilly.

As she was walking back, Hope could hear her cell phone ringing. She quickly ran to grab it from the kitchen counter. It stopped. She looked at the caller ID. No, it was not the vet service. It was him. It was her boss, Mazdon Elliott. It was 7:01 a.m. Why was he calling her? And more, why was he calling her at 7:01 a.m.? Hope did not have time to return the call. She would text Lacie and let her know what was taking place.

Faith had positioned herself in a sitting position. Hope did not know if she could get her out of the crate or not. She needed something to coax her out. Hope headed to the refrigerator. Snacks. She needed a bribe. The cell phone buzzed again. Hope looked at the number as she passed. It was him, again. What in the world was so important that he had now called two times? He would just have to wait.

Hope opened the refrigerator door and went to grab a slice of cheese. That was all that was needed – the rustling of the plastic wrapping. Faith waddled towards Hope and plopped down and scratched her paw against Hope. "Good girl. I'll give you a little bite, and then, we need to get on our way." It took all the strength that Hope could muster to lift Faith and place her in the front seat. "Everything is going to be all right," Hope whispered into Faith's face. It had to be all right. There was no other outcome to be considered.

CHAPTER 11

Mazdon could not believe he could not get in contact with Hope. How difficult was it to pick your phone up and answer? Even more frustrating, she did not have voicemail set up. Who, in this day and age, does not have their voicemail set up? He needed to speak with her about the Bitty Bites Bakery campaign changes. They were not that drastic. Just a few more debut dates and social media postings needed to be added to the calendar. Mazdon told himself, *I'm going to attempt one more telephone call, and if nothing, then all hell is going to break loose.* He dialed. It began to ring, and then, he heard her voice.

Hope had arrived at Dr. Bayley's office. They knew that Faith may not be able to walk in on her own accord, so when Hope pulled in, the staff were already waiting with a rolling gurney. Hope hopped out and ran to the other side to assist. Faith was panting heavily. It as if she could not catch her breath. Hope had been worried, but now, she was scared. One of the vet techs told her a room had already been prepared for Faith. Dr. Bayley was waiting to begin the examination. The tech told her they would be doing x-rays and to see how the puppies were faring. Hope had learned from Dr. True that most female bulldogs necessitated a C-section. This was in large part because of the makeup of the bulldog. Hope did a last-minute check on the car and gathered her satchel that contained all of Faith's favorite stuffed toys and blanket. Hope did not know what was going to happen, but knew these would comfort Faith.

As she walked into Dr. Bayley's waiting area, Hope prayed. "Lord, I'm not in need, but she is. Please keep Faith under your protection as we bring new life into the world. Lord, we don't have time to waste. If you could just take it straight to the Holy Spirit, with very little explanation, it would be appreciated. Amen." Hope had learned this prayer from her mom when the known had become the unknown.

Hope needed to answer the questions that were listed on the intake. Attention to detail was waning. Hope finished and her cell began to ring. Not again. How many more times was he going to call? She had texted Lacie where she was, and if there were any problems that Lacie could not handle on her own to call Hope on her cell. Hope concluded he was not going to go away. Okay. Enough. Hope had no more patience. There was so much going on. Hope's mind was spinning with worry. She answered the phone with what she thought would deter any more calls. "Mazdon, if you want me, come get me." And then disconnected the call. That should take care of this morning's crisis, Hope thought to herself. Little did she know what was about to happen.

No, she did not just hang up on Mazdon. No, she did not just say what he thought she said. If you want me, come get me. Mazdon called Lacie immediately. He did give Lacie time to plead Hope's case. He instructed Lacie to give him the address of where Hope was, and he would drive there with the Bitty Bites Bakery campaign revisions. Lacie knew Hope would be upset, but the boss needed her. Who was Lacie to stand in the way of what the boss wanted? Lacie gave Mazdon the address. Mazdon thanked her and began the drive to ……. wait, where was he going? Lacie had only given him the address, not a name, not even the telephone number. Only the address. Mazdon googled the address to see how far he was from the location given. Fifteen minutes was the drive time. Mazdon would make it in ten. The drive over, all Mazdon could do was to keep replaying those words "if you want me, come get me." Why were these words now taking a different undertone with Mazdon?

What was the name of this place? Lacie did not give the name, but only the address. As Mazdon was driving towards the destination, he was contemplating how he was going to address the "if you want me, come get me" statement. What was going on? No one at the agency had mentioned anything, nor had he heard any office gossip. They were a tight-knit group. Mazdon had noticed that "they" were not forthcoming at the morning meeting with any information on Hope's personal life. Mazdon heard the GPS repeat the direction to turn right in 50 feet and the destination would be on the left. Where in the world was he driving to when he noticed – it was an animal hospital. Okay. Now, he was totally puzzled. Mazdon parked and walked toward the entrance. He did not know what was going to be behind the door when he opened them, but he felt he was going to be surprised.

He opened the door and looked in to see if he could see her. There were several in the waiting room. A man with a calico cat, a couple with their lab, and woman with her head down in her hands, with no animal. It was her. She was that woman. Mazdon walked towards her and sat down beside her. She did not even notice.

Hope could sense that someone had sat down beside her. She was just too worried to look up. She just could not deal with any questions. She was about ready to break into tears if the staff did not come out and tell her what was taking place. If felt like she had been waiting for hours, when in actuality, she knew it had been fifteen minutes. Hope was not sure who was sitting beside her, but there was a familiarity. She turned her head sideways to glance from the side. Her heart fell. It was her boss. It was Mazdon Elliott, in the flesh. She could not look at him. This could only mean trouble. And she remembered those last words she said to him. "If you want me, come get me." Lawd, he took her up on that statement. Before she could think any further, she heard him ask, "Hope, is there anything you want to tell me? I'm going to say this is a good time for you to share a bit of what is occurring right now."

Hope looked at him. "It's rather simple. Please listen, as I do not have the time to explain all that has taken place over the past three days." And so, she began. "Returning from my parents' house, I saw a truck throw a box to the ditch. I stopped. It was an animal. I drove to the nearest shelter. I was told it was a female bulldog and that she was going to have babies. I could have left her there at the shelter, or I could adopt and take her with me. I chose the latter. Dr. True told me Faith was due any day. And when it happened, it would need to be C-section. We woke up this morning, and Faith was panting. I called Dr. Bayley. They said to bring her in for examination. Here I am. What brings you to my neck of the woods?" Hope could not wait to hear his response. She had meant that last statement to be sarcastic. She was overcome with worry about Faith.

Mazdon nodded. "I was curious, and now, I am curious no longer. Is there anything that I can do?"

Just as Hope was about to tell him what he could do, Dr. Bayley opened the door and walked into the lobby. "Hope, let's go into my office. We need to discuss what is going on with Faith." Hope stood up. Her legs felt weak. She reached back for the arm seat. Mazdon caught her. He whispered to where only she could hear his words, "I don't want you to say anything. I am going back there with you." Hope did not have the gumption to argue with him.

She waved her hand in the air. "Fine. Let's go."

Mazdon followed Hope down the hallway to where the vet's office was. He told them both to have a seat. He addressed them as Mr. and Mrs. Sloan. Hope opened her mouth and felt Mazdon's hand touch her arm. "Go ahead, Dr. Bayley."

"I am concerned that we cannot wait. We need to do the C-section within the next hour. I cannot take the chance of losing the babies or losing Faith. I need your permission to schedule." A tear formed in the corner of Hope's eye. This was not how the day was supposed to go. Hope was not ready.

And then she heard Mazdon say, "We agree with all that we have been advised. What time is the surgery?"

Dr. Bayley nodded his head. "Good. I will give you fifteen minutes to see her."

Hope could not look at Mazdon. She was going to cry. She was feeling overwhelmed. She was scared. She was afraid. She took a deep breath and began to shake. Mazdon had never seen his assistant vice president so fragile. Hope Sloan was always in control. Mazdon did the only thing he knew to do. He pulled her into his chest. He gently pushed her hair away from her face and kissed her forehead. "Everything will be fine. Remember, you said if I wanted you to come get you. I am here right now. I am not going anywhere." Hope sniffled and nodded. Mazdon reached for her pinkie and entwined his within hers. Dr. Bayley rose and told Mazdon and Hope to follow him. Mazdon and Hope walked down the corridor together. "She's right in here. We've just given her the anesthesia. She will be a bit out of it, but she will know you are there. All will be well."

He opened the doors and told Mazdon and Hope to put on the scrubs that had been left, and to follow him. Mazdon told Hope to turn around and he would tie her scrubs and then, she could tie his. The operating room doors opened to allow them entry. Hope felt her eyes crinkle. The tears were forming. Mazdon was observing Hope.

Hope leaned in and whispered to Faith, "Please, Lord, watch over her. Keep the babies safe." She then kissed the bullie on her squooshie face. "I will never leave you."

Dr. Bayley assured Hope and Mazdon that as soon as Faith and the babies were in recovery, they could come back again. He did not understand why, but in that moment, Mazdon knew that his life was about to change forever.

CHAPTER 12

Eternity. That's what it felt like. Two hours had passed. Hope started twisting in her chair.

Mazdon did the only thing he knew. He placed his hand on Hope's arm. "Let's get some air. Go ahead and check with the front desk and see how things are progressing. Then we will go outside to stretch, okay?"

Hope nodded. His touch had sent a warmth through her. This feeling was foreign. She did not know if she could stand or not. What was going on? Why was she reacting this way? She walked to the desk, and they informed her that Dr. Bayley had not come out to inform them of anything. If he did, they would come get her.

Hope turned and looked at Mazdon. She shook her head back and forth. "Nothing, yet," Hope informed him.

Mazdon opened the doors that led outside. He placed his hand on the small of her waist. As they walked outside, without any warning, Hope stopped and turn into Mazdon's chest and began to sob. "I cannot do this, Mazdon. I have no idea how to be a mom. I have no idea how to take care of all these puppies. I have bitten off more than I can chew. What was I thinking? I just couldn't leave her. She needed me. I could not leave her." She was rambling and she couldn't stop. "I'm sorry. I am just a bit overwhelmed."

Mazdon pulled back and placed his hand under her chin, so she would have to look at him. "It's okay. Slow down just a bit. We will get this lined out and taken care of. Faith will be fine, and so will the puppies. Let's go back in and make the 'to do' list. Deal?"

Hope sniffled. She heard his comment, specifically that word "we". Why she felt better, she could not fathom. She agreed. As they turned to walk back in, Dr. Bayley was standing outside the entry door. "Ya'll good out here?"

Hope smiled. "Yes, sir."

"Good, then. You can now go back and see Faith and the four beautiful puppies that have been delivered. There are two boys and two girls. Faith is a bit out of it, due to the anesthesia. The puppies are being cleaned and will be ready to nurse."

Hope hugged Mazdon. And in return, he hugged her back. He did not want to let her go. She fit rather nicely into his chest, and his arms held her tight. "Thank you, Mazdon. I know you had no idea what you were getting into."

Mazdon stated over her head, as he was still holding her, "Let's go see your new family."

Hope could not believe it. Faith was laying on a pet mattress that would accommodate her body and allow nursing for the puppies. Hope turned to be sure that Mazdon was still beside her. "Can you believe it? Just look at them. They are my babies." Mazdon could not contain his grin. He could not help but watch Hope as she kissed Faith. Faith returned the kiss by licking Hope. And what was that unusual sound. He wrapped his arms around Hope's waist. He leaned in close to Hope's face.

"Listen to them, they are making such cute noises," Hope informed him. So that's what that was. The puppies were nursing. And rather loudly.

Dr. Bayley walked in. "The surgery went well. There is a total of four. Two little girls and two little boys. We would like to keep Faith and the puppies for two nights, to be sure that the stitches remain and are healing, and that the puppies are getting enough milk. Hope, you can visit any time you want." Hope nodded in agreement. She wanted the very best for Faith and this would allow her time to prepare her home for Faith's return with the new family members.

CHAPTER 13

Hope was elated. She was on top of the mountain with relief and also trepidation. She needed to do a lot of preparation and shopping for products to bring all these fur babies to her home. As she and Mazdon were walking to the car, something was not right. She did not feel right. She turned to see where he was, and then all she could see was Mazdon running towards her.

He saw her ahead of him. She looked a bit wobbly with her walk. It dawned on him that neither he nor she had eaten while at the vet's office. He was going to insist before he returned her home that they stop and grab a quick bite. Before he could mention that idea though, Hope had another. He saw her turn, and Mazdon knew she was going to fall to the ground. How quickly could he get to her?

Hope began to fall, and then she was lifted up. She was pulled against his chest. And all she heard was, "I knew I should have fed you." She heard the click of the car door. He placed her up against the car with one hand and opened the door and positioned her on the seat. "Hope Sloan, don't you dare pass out on me. Open those pretty brown eyes, so I can see you are comprehending what I'm saying," Mazdon begged her.

Hope did as she was commanded. "I hear you and see you, Mazdon. Stop fretting. You'll put wrinkles on your forehead."

Mazdon laughed. "I don't want to hear one word. We are going to get something to eat. I think you're feeling a bit lightheaded from not eating or drinking anything since we brought Faith in. Let's go to the sandwich shop just a couple blocks down. And even though it's just down the block, we are driving, and I will be driving."

Hope wanted to argue the case of walking instead of driving, but she truly was tired. "Fine, fine. I will give into you on this one, but only this one," Hope told him.

The sandwich shop was—oh, what was that word her mom and dad would have come up with? "Quaint". It was quaint. The name made it even more so – "Love You A Latte". Best of all, it smelled like chocolate, which reminded Hope of her mom. Right now, with everything that had taken place since returning, Hope needed her mom. She knew her mom would make everything all right.

She turned to Mazdon. "I did not realize it until the aroma hit me, I am famished, Mazdon."

He smiled. "Me, too. Feel free to order whatever your heart desires. It's on me," Mazdon replied. She stopped to tell Mazdon he did not need to do that, but instead, she ran right smack dab into his chest. Mazdon caught her, so she would not stumble. He looked down at Hope. "I got you."

There was no explanation that Hope could come up with as to why she started blushing. You could not slide a piece of paper between Hope and Mazdon. That's how close their bodies were touching. Hope inhaled the scent of Mazdon. As Mazdon was watching for a reaction from Hope, he came to the realization that holding Hope in his arms was have a certain effect on him. He could smell her perfume. It smelled of orchids and vanilla.

That took Mazdon back to a comment he remembered his father had made: "The essence of work is not just the commitment, but the time and effort given to the commitment. Never allow any one individual to interrupt the journey or the path that you must take. There are times that you will need to walk alone." This was one of the reasons Mazdon had never seriously dated or held a relationship longer than two months. He only had time for the ad agency.

He gently pushed Hope away and pointed towards a table near the window that was available. Their orders were taken. The sandwich, pasta salad, sweet tea and—of course—the slice of cheesecake were all that was needed to revive Hope's mission. She needed to go shopping at the nearest pet store and gather all items necessary to bring Faith and the puppies home.

"Mazdon, I just want you to know I appreciate everything you have done. You have gone out of your way with kindness. But I think I can take it from here. The day is not over, and I still need to get all the supplies necessary to bring Faith home. I cannot ask you to do one more thing. I do hope you can understand."

Mazdon did not know whether to laugh at how fast Hope had made that statement without taking one breath or missing a beat or more to be relieved he was off the hook for the remainder of the day. Yet, he did not want to leave Hope. He was enjoying himself. He could not remember when the last time was that he had taken a day off from work without thinking about work. Funny how that happened.

He reached across the table and touched her hand. "It's okay. I really do not mind. Everything is okay back at the agency. Plus, you may need a man around to assist with loading and unloading all the supplies," Mazdon told her. Before Hope could make a snarky reply about "need a man", their food was delivered. It looked delicious. She was too hungry to argue. First, she would eat, then, she would argue with Mazdon.

CHAPTER 14

Mazdon had paid for the meal. Hope told him it was not necessary, but he insisted. Walking towards the vehicle, Hope admitted she did need his help. Having more than one body to help with the list would make the day more productive. She looked at Mazdon, who was watching her. "Is there something on my face, Mazdon? You've been staring at me."

Mazdon had been watching her. He came to the realization he did not know who Hope Sloan was. Today, she had exhibited strength and endurance in dealing with the female bulldog, Faith. No wonder she was at the top of Spotlight Marketing Agency. For the first time in a long time, Mazdon saw what he would want in relationship. Why now?

They got into the vehicle and began the journey to the pet supply store. Walking inside, Hope told Mazdon she had the list, and if they could each take a cart and half of the list, the collection of items would go much faster than if she were alone. He nodded. She rolled the cart towards him and handed him half the paper. "One more thing, just to make it interesting, whoever finishes their list first wins."

"Wins what?" Hope asked him smiling.

"That's for me to know and you to find out. Ready, set, go!"

Mazdon knew Hope would not turn down the challenge. He knew that she was competitive. That was why she was the lead on the big campaigns. He pulled his piece of paper out and waved it in the air. He was teasing Hope. She hated to lose, and she was not going to lose to her boss, that was for darn sure. Hope viewed the list briefly and took off. Mazdon watched her as she wheeled down the lane. She may be the best team leader at the agency, but he was not going to give her any leeway.

Mazdon finished and was checking out with all the items on his list. He had pushed the cart to the end, so the clerk could bag everything, when he noticed her standing there with a big smile on her face. It was not just a smile; it was a smile of victory. He had been beaten. How? How in the world did she finish before him?

Mazdon was unloading their carts and watching Hope from the corner of his eye. She was smiling and humming. He did not understand, but he was enjoying this moment. Hope knew he was staring. She could feel his eyes. She did not mind for some reason. They had been together most of the day, and Mazdon had been nothing but supportive. Nothing like she would have imagined outside the office. Maybe there was more to him than met the eye. No one on the agency team would believe her. She started laughing.

Mazdon stopped in midstream with dog bed in his arms. "And pray tell, Miss Hope Sloan, what do you find so funny?"

Hope grinned. "You, Mazdon Elliott. Here I thought you were an ogre, a tyrant, a no-feeling kind of guy, and you have spent more than half the day with me, helping me. Who are you?"

Mazdon made sure all items were loaded. He winked at Hope. "Let's get you home, and we will get the nursery established." Hope could not utter a word. Who had taken her boss, and where did they put him? She heard the word "we", and that stopped her in her tracks.

"Correct me if I am wrong: I did hear you say 'we', didn't I?"

Mazdon shook his head. "Yes, Hope, I am going to help. No biggie."

She was walking to the side of her car and reached for the door handle. At the same time, Mazdon was reaching to open Hope's door handle as well. His hand was not moving. Hope did not know what was happening, but Mazdon's touch had sent a fire through her that she had never experienced. What in the world was going on? And why did Hope not want to let go of the door handle?

"Hope, if you want to get inside, I need you to move your hand." Mazdon could tell. She had felt it. He had felt it. Hope began to blush. Mazdon thought how vulnerable she looked. Instinct kicked in. He wanted to protect Hope. From what, he did not know. She was seated and buckled in. He started his vehicle and then remembered. He would need to return her to the vet's to retrieve her car, or he would have to pick her up in the morning to take her back. He did not want to return her to the vet. He wanted to spend more time with Hope, plus she would need his assistance in unloading the pet supplies and establishing the makeshift nursery for Faith and her puppies.

He turned to Hope, and before he could rethink his decision, he told her, "I know you don't need my help, but I do not have anything planned for the remainder of the day, and I don't mind at all." As Hope was listening to his explanation, she did not want him to return her to the vet. She could do it alone, but it would be nice to have his assistance in carrying the larger items. Besides that, she liked his company.

Hope placed her hand on his. "Thank you. That would be nice." Time *stopped*. Time stood still, and so did Hope and Mazdon. She was frozen. She could not remove her hand from his.

Unknowingly, Mazdon turned his hand to squeeze Hope's. "It's okay, Hope, to tell me that you only want me for my muscles and not my beauty. I understand. I'll be okay. No hard feelings." Mazdon was teasing her. They both looked at each other, and at the same time, they burst into laughter. "Well, at least, you understand my intentions. Hopefully, I've made them clear as mud to you," Hope told him. Mazdon could not fathom how this conversation had turned the tables on him.

"Then, it's agreed. I'll take you home and help you unload. You can get some rest, and then, I will swing by and pick you up in the morning to get Faith and the puppies." Mazdon held his hand out for Hope to shake. Catching him off guard, Hope hugged him and laid her face on his chest. "Thank you, Mazdon. I don't know how I would have been able to handle today without your kindness."

Mazdon did not want to move. She belonged here. She fit here. He had not had feelings like this for a long time. He placed his hands on the sides of her arm and pulled her back a bit, so he could see her face. She was vulnerable. He could tell she was not just tired, but she was boogered out. With no thought of what may happen, he kissed her on the forehead.

What had she just done? Had she lost her ever-loving mind? He was her boss. She was his employee. She had crossed the line. Shoot, she had even crossed the tracks. He was looking at her. Hope knew he was going to kiss her. She did not want to leave his embrace. She was ready. And then. He kissed her on the forehead. No, he did not. Not the forehead. No lips. No cheek. Nothing but the forehead. Seriously?

Before she could contemplate what may or may not happen next, Mazdon informed her in a very husky voice that the vehicle was loaded, and they needed to get her home and begin the preparations. Hope told Mazdon, "Fine." As she was buckling her seatbelt, her only thought was that he had ONLY kissed her on the forehead.

The silence in the car could have been pierced with a knife. Mazdon could only think about the kiss. He should not have even kissed Hope on the forehead. His only saving grace was the fact that were it anything else, except the forehead, he would be in trouble. He wanted to taste the kisses from her lips. Thank goodness he had the sense to pull away.

Hope could not find the words to discuss anything in the car. She was still reeling from the fact that he had ONLY kissed her forehead. She recognized that she had wanted more. What in the world was happening? It could be the stress that she was under. It could be the fact that she was lonely. She could come up with a million reasons at this point, but it boiled down to the fact that there was an attraction between both of them. Hope wondered if he was reminiscing over that kiss.

They approached Hope's home. Mazdon turned into the driveway. To his surprise, Hope's home looked very inviting. Of course, it was still the winter and the landscaping had that "tarnished" look to it, but it was neat. The front porch had make-believe fencing. On one side was a swing that hung from the top. On the other side were a table and two chairs. If someone wanted to share dinner while watching the sun fade, this would be the perfect spot.

Mazdon looked over at Hope. She had her hand on the doorknob. "I tell you what, Hope. Go ahead and unlock the front door. I'll start bringing everything to the porch, and you can get it inside, and then, we will set up all that is needed to bring Faith and the puppies home. Does that sound like a plan?" She nodded in agreement. She still could not get the words out. She so wanted to ask, "And that was it?" She walked the sidewalk, stepped to the porch, and unlocked the door. Hope needed a moment to gather her emotions. In all the years, she had worked for Spotlight Marketing Agency, her boss had never ever been to her home. Yet, here he was. And he had muscles. Taut muscles under his shirt. Hope could see as he was lifting the pet supplies. He was rather …. what was the word her mom used? It's the word Hope's mom used to describe Hope's dad on their first date— he was rather "fetching". Hope held the door wide, so that Mazdon could have access to the living room for the items.

As the last item was laid down, Mazdon sensed that Hope was overwhelmed by the way she had been pacing since she had gotten home. "Hope," he began. "Stop for just a minute. Let's rest. I don't know about you, but I am tired. I'm whooped. It's been a day for both you and I." Hope wanted to argue that she was not tired, but, in fact, stopping for just a moment sounded really good. Hope asked if Mazdon wanted some sweet tea or bottled water. Mazdon could not remember the last time he had drank sweet tea, but he was game. She brought the drink to him. Without hesitation, Mazdon took a swig. It was the best sweet tea he had tasted in a long time. Just like his mom used to make. Amazing how a small drink such as this could bring back those memories of his mom.

Hope had already sat down on the couch. She patted the couch and told him, "Sit for a spell." Mazdon did not need her to tell him twice. "I figure if we rest for a bit, we can finish the set-up in about an hour. Is that okay with you?"

Mazdon nodded. "We are on your time, lovely lady."

Hope nodded. "I just need to close my eyes. I'll turn the TV on, and you can flip the remote until you find a show you like." Mazdon very rarely had the time to watch TV. He was always on the go and thinking about potential clients and ways to entice them to the Spotlight Marketing Agency. Shoot, maybe he would enjoy watching a few minutes of sports or a series. Hope handed him the remote. Mazdon started flipping the channels. *Typical man*, Hope thought. He only allowed two seconds before he started flipping to another station.

How in the world could you enjoy a show if all you did was keep it on that station for two seconds? You just couldn't have time to find out what was taking place. She smiled. And before she knew it, her eyes had closed.

Mazdon did not have a clue as to what shows, movies, or series were on TV. He could not find anything that piqued his interest for more than two seconds. He felt something soft against his shoulder and turned his head to see her. Hope had fallen asleep on his shoulder. He knew if he moved, he would wake her up. Then it came to him. When was the last time he, himself, had actually taken a nap during the day? If he leaned his body towards the end of the couch arm, her body would have to follow his leaning, and then, both of them could get some shut eye. He probably wouldn't go to sleep. He pulled the pillow close to him and leaned his head down, and sure enough, her body did the same. As if it were supposed to be right where it was. She fit nicely into the silhouette of Mazdon's body. So much so it was too perfect. This was not good. He positioned himself so that he was able to pick her up in his arms. She curled into his chest. He located her bedroom. It was not frilly. It was Hope. The bed was a beautiful cherry sleigh bed with colors of burgundy, forest green, and gold. There were quilts in the corner on a rocking chair. Hope's dresser held pictures of what Mazdon assumed were her and her parents. In the corner was the entry to the bathroom, accentuated in the same colors. Mazdon lay Hope down on the bed and walked to the rocking chair. He grabbed a quilt and lay it across Hope.

There was no reason to stay, but yet, he could not leave her. He grabbed two more quilts and walked back to the living room. The couch did look inviting. He would only sleep for an hour or less. As he laid his head down, his last thoughts were, *There's more to Hope Sloan than meets the eye.*

CHAPTER 15

Hope turned to see the sun shining through her blinds. What time was it? And then she looked down and realized she was in her bed. How did she get here? Better yet, who put her in the bed? She remembered she told Mazdon she just needed to close her eyes. Little did she expect to be knocked out until the morning of the next day. The house had not been readied for Faith and the puppies. Hope needed to shower, fix some hot tea and a toast/egg sandwich, and then get the day started. She jumped in the shower. It felt great to just stand under the raining water. She had not realized how much she needed this time. Everything moved so quickly and a bit out of control. She stepped out and slipped on her t-shirt and shorts. No need to put on a bra or panties. She would not be seeing anyone this morning until she made the call to Dr. Bayley. She walked to the kitchen. She plugged in the toaster and turned the burner on the oven. Hope had placed the carton of eggs to the side counter. She was getting ready to break the egg when she heard, "I was going to make breakfast for you. Do you still need help? Because if not, can I place my order?"

Hope screamed. The egg in her hand was thrown into the air and splatted everywhere. "Are you joking? Where in the world did you come from? And better yet, how long have you been on my couch?"

Mazdon went to sleep as soon as his head hit the decorated pillow that was on Hope's couch. He knew he should have probably driven home, but if he did, there would have been a lot of noise while trying to leave as quietly as possible. He was not a quiet person. So Mazdon decided on the latter. Just sleep on the couch. Not the most comfortable choice, but the obvious choice.

Mazdon knew she was stirring. He heard the bed shift and then the shower was turned on. He would get up in a few minutes and begin breakfast for both of them. There was only one problem with that idea. He had no idea what Sloan ate for breakfast. Shoot, the only time he had seen Hope eat any kind of food was yesterday when they ate at Love You A Latte. And even then, she did not eat a whole lot. So Mazdon decided to stay put until he could personally ask her himself.

"You! Where are your clothes, and what in God's name are you doing here?" Hope stammered on these words. He was naked. No, not all the way naked, but halfway. Either way, she could not look him in the face.

What was even worse, she could not remove her eyes from his chest. And there was no way she was going to have her eyes travel down. She was turning red. She could feel it. Her entire being was turning red, and she couldn't stop it. Mazdon stopped less than a foot from her. He knew she was shaken by his presence. He also could see she was blushing. He was enjoying her unsettling. Mazdon had never known this side of his assistant vice president, but Hope Sloan was very attractive. In this moment, she was too enticing. She was wearing a matching tee and shorts in hot pink polka dots. Mazdon was grinning. Hope wanted to wipe that grin off his face.

Right now, she needed his help in cleaning up the egg that was laid out on the kitchen floor.

CHAPTER 16

"Mazdon Elliott, you need to get dressed. You can't be in my kitchen with no clothes on." Mazdon wondered if she knew how she sounded. "I will help you clean this up. Get me a rag and mop, and I'll take care of it while you finishing cooking. May I ask you for a cup of hot tea as well, and if you can handle cracking some more eggs without pitching them in the air like a baseball, I would like an egg and a piece of toast, pretty please."

Hope giggled. It was not a laugh. It was a giggle, and she could not stop. Within five minutes of walking from her bedroom to the kitchen, her day had been tossed in the air, much like the egg. It seemed so apropos with everything else that was taking place. She placed her hands on the counter, looking at Mazdon with the best stern look she could muster without smiling, "Absolutely, Mazdon, I'll get right on our breakfast. It would be my pleasure."

Mazdon walked over to where the mess was. He looked at Hope. He tapped his finger on her nose. "I apologize. Where are my manners? I forgot to tell you good morning."

Before Hope could respond, Mazdon kissed her on the forehead. She did not pull back. She leaned into the kiss. She leaned into Mazdon. This was not just Mazdon, but her boss. She steadied herself by placing her hands on each of side of Mazdon. She could tell his arms were not only strong, they were muscular and well-defined.

Before Hope could decide to ask what he was doing, Mazdon's thumb was wreaking havoc on Hope's lips. He had taken the liberty of tracing her lips. Hope took a breath in. She dare not make any movement. In reality, she knew she could not move. Mazdon had caught her off guard by being on the couch, but this kiss had sent her head spinning. She had no clue as to what she should do. For the first time ever, Hope had no plan. She had nothing except her employer / boss, Mazdon Elliott, standing in front of her.

Mazdon did not know what had come over him. She was standing there being indignant and looking so sexy at the same time. Mazdon knew she had no clue how titillating she looked at this moment. He could not help but kiss her forehead, and then, he could not stop.

The pertinent pout of her lips drew the desire to trace them with his thumb. Each stroke placed heightened his awareness of Hope and the precarious situation they had both been placed in. He slowly leaned in to touch her lips with his. He only required a nibble, as if to say good morning. He caught the upper part of her lip and began to gently tug at the corner. With each suckling motion, he pulled her lips closer to his. This was not how he had planned the day to begin, but he did not want to stop. He did not want to think of anything else but the woman who stood before him. In that moment, Mazdon knew that Hope Sloan was not just his assistant vice president, she was breathtaking. Why he had never seen this before was beyond his comprehension. He only knew he needed more.

Hope closed her eyes and felt the caressing of her lips with Mazdon's thumb. Light, feathery strokes placed upon her bottom lip. Hope knew her lips were swollen from his touch. Hope could not recall ever feeling this way. A fire was in his touch. She opened her lips for Mazdon. She invited him to taste what she had held back from so many others. Unknowingly, his hands reached for Hope. He pulled her tighter to his chest. Hope could feel Mazdon's heart beating fast. He placed one hand on the small of her back and began to rub in circular motions just above the waist of her shorts. The room was spinning. Hope was lightheaded. She could only hold on to Mazdon tighter to keep herself from falling.

"I have you Hope. I won't let you fall", Mazdon told her. "I've wanted to kiss you, Hope Sloan, since this morning watching you fret. Now I know why you were behaving the way you were." Hope looked astonished. He had noticed she was out of sorts.

She was tired. Trying to keep this secret was wearing her out. "I did my best to conceal the secret— or at least I thought I did", Hope commented.

What happened next neither anticipated. Mazdon could not resist, listening to her plead her case. He leaned into Hope and said "open your lips for me again." Hope did not want to and opened her mouth to tell Mazdon no, but instead her body betrayed her and leaned into Mazdon, close enough for his lips to touch hers. His lips were strong. They were not soft. They were demanding. Hope inhaled and opened her mouth to allow his tongue to enter. He swirled his tongue around Hope's until she could not breathe. Small motions of in and out and then circling her tongue with his. Her tongue had never been used in such a passionate form. Mazdon moved his mouth towards the side of Hope's neck. He nibbled his way down her shoulder and then his hand came up to gently remove it off to the side. Her shoulder was exposed and Mazdon took full advantage of placing kisses here. He felt the change in her body as she responded. Mazdon took his other hand, and even though the t-shirt was still on, he found her erect nipple and began to rub it between his thumb and finger.

Hope arched her back. Mazdon began the kisses to the other side and continued the teasing of Hope's nipple. There was a pain that shot through Hope. One that was not of hurt, but one that was enveloped with need. She needed a release, and here he was. Her boss was standing in front of her, making love to her in the morning in her kitchen. She should stop, but desire had consumed all logic. For the first time in a very long time, Hope felt desired. Mazdon's desire could be felt against Hope. She shivered. Mazdon sensed the change in her. This could be all wrong or could be all right. Mazdon picked Hope up before she knew what was taking place. He placed her on top of the kitchen counter and placed his face in between her breasts. Lawd, she smelled of sweet honey.

CHAPTER 17

Hope's cell phone began vibrating on the kitchen table. Mazdon stepped back. Hope looked at Mazdon and then at her phone. There could only be two individuals who would be calling this early in the morning. One would be work and the other would be the vet's office. Hope peeked at the number. It was, indeed, the vet's office. She picked it up and said, "Hello."

That hello sent Mazdon into action. He began cleaning up the floor where the egg had been dropped. He could hear Hope asking questions. How soon could she pick Faith and the puppies up? What was the expense of the delivery? The sooner the kitchen was put back in order, Mazdon could be on his way. He did not want to discuss what had just transpired in Hope Sloan's kitchen.

Hope was watching him out of the corner of her eye. Whatever in the world was he doing? She was trying to concentrate on Dr. Bayley's instructions and good report of Faith and the puppies, and he was on the floor with wet paper towels cleaning the mess up. Her attention span was all over the place. Between him, the egg, and the call, Hope was on the verge on tears. Tears of frustration. She hated when her anxiety got the best of her. She needed a few minutes to collect herself. In reality, she knew this was not going to happen, at least not this morning.

She laid the phone down and cleared her throat. "Mazdon, you do not have to do that. I need to go shower. Faith and the puppies are ready to be picked up. Thank you for all your help and kindness, but I believe I have asked too much of you."

Mazdon smiled. She sounded so business-like and professional. Just like being at work. This was the side he was used to seeing. Leaving Hope to fend for herself would not be a problem. He threw the rest of the paper towels in the trash can. He deliberately took his time as he walked towards Hope. Within inches of those lips he had just suckled, he whispered "Hope, you have not asked enough of me, but that's to be discussed later. If you need me, you have my cell. You just need to call."

Hope raised her voice. She did not need to whisper her anger. "Never. I will not need you any more, Mr. Elliott. I am quite capable of handling Faith and the puppies on my own. Again, thank you for what you have done."

Mazdon nodded. "I can assume I will see you at work this morning, on time." Mazdon knew the answer to this. There was no way in heaven that Hope could arrive to work at her normal scheduled timeframe. Hope knew what he was trying to do. He did not think her capable of taking care of Faith and the puppies all by herself, and arrive on time at work. He was baiting her, and it was working. She wanted to wipe that all-knowing grin off his face. She would need additional time to take care of Faith and get all the puppies set up for the day. But that was not all of it. Dr. Bayley had informed Hope that Faith and the puppies would require 24-hour around-the-clock care for the first two weeks. Hope was doomed. She was going to have to request time off work. She needed maternity leave in order to take care of Faith and the pups.

And then, it hit her. She could work from home. She would have the office VPN her in, and if she needed to hold a meeting, the team could come to her via ZOOM. It was a win-win for all. With modern-day technology, there was no need for Hope to miss any assignments or campaigns.

Hope turned towards Mazdon. "Mr. Elliott, I have a proposition for you. Both you and I know that I do need time to take care of the situation with Faith and the pups. You are well aware of this. Because you now know and have heard that I need the time, I would like to request furternity leave."

Mazdon stopped in his tracks. "I'm sorry, Hope. What did you say? What type of leave do you need?"

"Instead of maternity leave, Mazdon, I need furternity leave. I have to take care of these puppies for a few weeks, in addition to Faith. I do have vacation hours that I can use. We can call it what you want. Vacation or furternity leave. You make the choice." Mazdon knew she was serious. This was a first for him. There had been only a few who had used the benefit of maternity leave, but never in his career had he heard of furternity leave.

"Hope, it's not that easy. We have meetings and new clients with expectations for their campaign. Your team needs you. I need you." Mazdon stated as a matter of fact.

"Mazdon, my mind is made up. I will not abandon Hope. She was thrown from a truck and left for dead. I will take care of her and the pups. I will go to HR today before going to pick her up from Dr. Bayley. I will request to use all my vacation days. I would rather not do that. I would offer the suggestion of having me work from home and do meetings either via ZOOM or to be held at my home. I need to take furternity leave."

They could go on like this, arguing back and forth about "furternity leave", or Hope could get on the road and take care of matters. Mazdon could tell she was anxious to pick up Faith and the pups. He would give her today off. She could use vacation time. When he arrived at work, he, too, would check with HR to determine how many hours she had accumulated or saved. He did not want any more surprises.

Hope could tell he was analyzing the predicament they were both in. Mazdon stated with calmness, "Fine, go ahead and call the office. Tell them you are taking a vacation day. We both will meet with HR later this week. Pick up Faith and the pups. I'll call you later with any fires that need to be put out."

Before she could think about her actions, she walked towards Mazdon and leaned up and kissed him on the side of his cheek. "Thank you, Mazdon."

She walked towards the bedroom, where he knew her bathroom was. Hope hollered at Mazdon, while walking into her bedroom, that there was another bathroom, where he could shower. She closed her door and disappeared.

Mazdon stood still for a moment. Actually, it was more than a moment. Did she just brush him off? Who was she? Within less than 24 hours, his entire world had been flipped like a pancake by this young woman who he had barely knew existed until yesterday. No one would believe him. He walked towards the spare bathroom. Mazdon looked through the cabinets to find a wash rag and towel. He noticed that if he were going to shower, he would be smelling like vanilla ice cream. This was the only body wash he could find. There was no bar of soap. There was the vanilla ice cream body wash, along with the matching shampoo and conditioner. Mazdon knew for a fact that someone would comment on his aroma. There was no way to disguise the scent. Mazdon did not have time to return to his home and shower. Better just do it and get it over with.

Hope opened her bedroom door. She was dressed in casual jeans and her favorite tee with her tennies. He was nowhere to be seen, but he had showered. She smiled. She smelled vanilla. He had to use what was in the spare bathroom. Served him right. Hope grabbed her purse and took one last look around her living room. She needed to call the office and request a vacation day. Yes, Faith was about to change her life.

CHAPTER 18

Mazdon parked and walked into the agency. There was a lot to be done. Mazdon had a meeting at 10:00 a.m. with a potential client wanting to grow his family's business known as "Pupsicles – Not Just for Pups". Mazdon was unsure if this was for the animal only, or if the humans could consume said product. He walked in and began the routine of check-in at the receptionist desk with Andee to see he had any messages. He walked to his office and closed the door. He sat down. That was a mistake. He began to think about the previous 24 hours. He could not help but wonder if Hope had picked Faith and the pups up yet. Would she have everything prepared to bring them home? What if she needed something and could not leave her home?

"Enough," Mazdon stated out loud. He knew he could not do anything until after the morning appointment with Pupsicles. He needed to concentrate on that and that alone. He buzzed Lacie to bring in the file, so they could both review it and note any particulars that needed to be asked before the pitch.

Lacie overhead Mazdon on her assistant's speaker phone. Good lawd, she was dreading a meeting with him. No one had heard a peep out of Mazdon since he had left in a huff to find Hope. She was jumping from the pot right into the fire. Lacie had tried to call Hope several times this morning, but no answer. Lacie knew what she was doing. Hope had a way of fading into the background, where she knew no one would look. Lacie felt this is what she needed to be doing, as well. Fading into the background, but Mazdon was not going to allow that to happen. Especially this day, with another big potential campaign and client. The walk from Lacie's office to Mazdon's office felt like a child who knew the punishment was coming and was trying to delay it as much as possible.

Lacie knocked, and she heard Mazdon state, "Come in." When she opened his office door, she had no idea what to expect, but it was not the man behind the desk. Even though dressed in a suit for the office, Mazdon Elliott looked a wee bit tired. Actually, he looked as if needed a nap. Lacie smiled. She was definitely going to ride by and stop at Hope's home. What in the dickens had occurred within such a short amount of time that could dishevel Mazdon?

Mazdon began the meeting with several bulleted items that would need a tweaking. Nothing major, but he wanted to have two alternatives to offer the potential client. The meeting took less than ten minutes. Lacie was shocked. He looked at her and said he would meet the team in the conference room at 9:50 a.m. to be sure that all was set and in place. Lacie nodded and arose.

Mazdon cleared his throat. "Lacie, has she called you this morning with any status updated on her situation? And before you panic, I know about the 'situation' with the bulldog and her newborn pups." Lacie told him no and stated she had tried to reach Hope, but she was not answering her cell. Mazdon then made a statement that Lacie knew something was definitely wrong with Mazdon. "After our meeting with Pupsicles and representatives, I'll be taking the rest of the day off." Lacie's eyes widened. "I'm sure you can complete whatever else is necessary to finalize Pupsicles. I have a good feeling about this potential client."

Lacie was *never* at a loss for words. This was an absolute first. "Yes, sir. I have this, Mazdon. Enjoy the afternoon. All will be taken care of. If I need you, I will, of course, text."

Mazdon could not understand why the need to see Hope was so critical. The anxiety of not knowing if Hope were okay, along with Faith and the puppies, was driving him a bit out of sorts. Mazdon was an "in control" kind of guy. Right now, he felt as if his world had been hit by a meteor and had shattered everywhere. He did not know which piece to pick up first. Before he started the vehicle, he made a call to Hope's cell. No answer. Was she ever going to set her voice mail up? Did she ever answer her flipping phone?

CHAPTER 19

Hope was on pins and needles as she walked into Dr. Bayley's office. The waiting room was filled to capacity. She walked to the receptionist and signed in. Hope's anxiety was at an all-time high. There were no empty seats. Hope stood to the side. The door opened and Dr. Bayley walked to the reception area, where all eyes turned to him. It was comical.

He started with, "Good morning everyone. Let's get this day started. Is Faith's mom in the room?" Hope stepped forward with a big smile. Dr. Bayley acknowledged and her and said, "Let's go see momma and those babies."

Hope immediately stepped forward and followed Dr. Bayley down the hallway, where Faith and the puppies would be waiting. Dr. Bayley stopped and turned. "Are you ready? Your entire world is about to change in just a matter of minutes."

Hope stopped. Could she do this? What if she could not? How was she going to manage Faith and the puppies? And the puppies needed good homes. Hope took a deep breath. He opened the door. Hope did not have time to even get one foot in the doorway when she heard Faith's pleading bark and the tip tap of nails on the floor. Faith planted herself right on Hope's foot. Hope leaned down and began to hug Faith.

Hope did not want to let go. Faith looked so good. And just like a proud mother, Faith turned and walked towards the puppies and then turned to be sure Hope was following. "I'm coming, baby girl. I know you want me to see them." Hope felt the first trickle begin down her cheek. Hope felt so many emotions in just that one second. She peered down into the play pen that had been made into a makeshift nursery. She counted them. Yes, four. Four perfect, precious baby bulldogs. Faith was sitting to the side of the playpen. Hope could sense she was waiting for Hope's approval. She kissed Faith on the top of her forehead.

Dr. Bayley cleared his throat. "Let's go over a few matters regarding the care of Faith and of the puppies. And then, you'll be good to go, and everyone can go home and begin a routine." Hope nodded, and Dr. Bayley gave her medications and paperwork with strict restrictions on the care of Faith and the puppies.

Hope picked up the small tub. The puppies were secure. There was no way they could escape. Hope had

Faith on a harness leash and walked her to the reception area. Payment needed to be made. Hope would get Faith set up in the car and then return for the puppies and to pay Dr. Bayley. She had all the medications in one arm, and Faith was leading the way to freedom while entangling Hope. Faith took off before Hope could balance herself.

A voice, all too familiar, said "I have you, Hope. Here, let me help you." Hope's heart skipped a beat. There was more behind this than wanting to help her. Something was going on, and she was going to get to the middle of Mazdon's surprise drop-in. Before she could though, she needed to get everything and everyone squared away.

She looked Mazdon square in the eye. "I don't believe you, but since you are standing there with nothing to do, can you please grab the puppies and follow me to my car? I just need to pay the bill, and Faith and I will be right behind you."

Mazdon laughed. "Oh, I have a lot to do, but right now, my entire focus is on you." Mazdon saw the puppies in the little tub and leaned down to check on them. Four little bulldog puppies. Mazdon did not have any pets. He was a true bachelor. There were no women and no pets that he was involved with. He could remember asking his father for a pet, but the request was always pushed to the side with some excuse regarding time, work, commitment, and responsibility. Mazdon eventually stopped asking.

Hope touched Mazdon's arm gently. "Are you ready, Mazdon? You seem a bit lost."

Mazdon shook it off. "I'm good, Hope. Lead the way. We'll follow."

CHAPTER 20

During the drive to her home, Hope could not help thinking about the events of the morning. She tried to call Lacie to get a feel for what had taken place at work. Of course, her voicemail box was full. Lawd, she needed to talk to Lacie about clearing messages out. She texted Lacie, but no response yet. She looked in her rear-view mirror. Yep, he was still there. He had not gotten lost. No wrong turns. Should she try to lose him? She started laughing hysterically. She couldn't stop herself. From the moment Hope had stopped to investigate the box she had seen thrown to the side of the road, her life had been turned inside out and upside down. One more thing or one more person added to the mix was no big deal, right?

Mazdon recalled where she lived. Mazdon could not forget about the past 24 hours with Hope Sloan. If he were honest with himself, he had never felt this way about someone. She was indignant. She was pushy. She was bossy. She was intelligent. AND, he was attracted to Hope Sloan. The kicker in this entire situation is that Hope probably had no clue of his feelings nor his intentions. Mazdon thoughts went to his intentions. What were his intentions with Hope Sloan? He gave thought to asking her out on date. That scenario did not fit her personality. More than likely, she would come up with an excuse about not having time because of Faith and the puppies, which he could understand. But there was no harm in surprising her with a home-cooked meal. *That* he might be able to pull off.

Hope put the car in park, undid her seatbelt, and leaned over to kiss Faith on the forehead in the passenger seat. The puppies were snug in their coverlet. Everything was going to be alright. It just had to be.

She knew he had already parked his vehicle and was walking towards her. She heard his footsteps. Before she could open the car door, he did so. He asked if she needed help with anything. Hope could not believe she was sitting in her car with her boss asking how he could help. The world was ending or might be. Hope was not sure of anything at this moment. She told him he could gather the puppies and bring them inside, so all could get acclimated to their new surroundings. He smiled and nodded. Hope made sure Faith got down out of the car without too much exertion. She looked over her shoulder to be sure that Mazdon had the carrier with the puppies safely in his arms. Dr. Bayley had told Hope that Faith would be tired and to let her just nurse the puppies as soon as they arrived home. A schedule would be needed for around-the-clock feedings. Hope was going to need more than herself. She needed an entire army.

She unlocked the front door, pushed the door open, and held it for Mazdon to walk through. She pointed to the den, where she had made a room for just Faith and the puppies. There was a small cot that Hope had placed in the room, so she could be close, if there was a need. Mazdon sat down on the floor. One by one, he placed the puppies in Hope's hands and watched her placed them carefully under the warming light. Hope looked at Mazdon. "Four, I counted four. We should be good to go." Mazdon heard the "we" before Hope realized she had said it. He rather liked she included him on this predicament of hers. "Let me feed Faith, and then, we will begin the nursing schedule, if that's okay with you," Hope told him.

Mazdon smiled. What was he going to do, say no? That wasn't likely, not with the way Hope was bossing him around. Mazdon sat on the floor staring at the puppies. All were huddled together, keeping each other company, as well as keeping each other warm. Faith was eating. As soon as he finished, he knew their job would begin.

He watched as Hope walked towards the bed that the puppies had been placed in. The incubator light was ready and on. Faith waddled nonchalantly over to her bed. She was full. Hope laughed and rubbed her belly as she lay sideways on her bed. She looked at Mazdon. "Well, don't just stand there. I'm hungry. I'm going to assume you are, as well. You know they are hungry. The sooner they get fed, the sooner we get fed. Pretty novel idea, wouldn't you say?"

Mazdon laughed. "As you desire, Ms. Sloan." He reached in and began handing the puppies to Hope. He watched as she gently laid each one to where they began to suckle. Faith was a natural mom. She laid peacefully still as her babies nursed. Mazdon was so intent on watching the puppies, he had forgotten Hope mentioned food.

He looked up. Hope was opening the refrigerator, all the while talking to Mazdon. He had not heard one word, but he politely acknowledged with a "yes". Time would tell what he said yes to. Hope turned and placed sandwiches and chips and two bottled waters on the kitchen table. "It's not much, but it may satisfy your appetite," Hope told Mazdon. Mazdon could not stop staring at Hope. She was an enigma. He could not put his finger on it, but he knew he did not want the evening to end.

As they ate, they shared small talk. There were no business questions. Hope began the conversation with "Did you have any pets growing up, Mazdon?"

Mazdon shook his head no. "My father never had the time nor the inclination for us to have a pet in our home. He was too busy to have to handle the care of me and the family business."

Hope touched Mazdon's hand. "I am sorry. You have missed out on the best thing a pet offers."

Mazdon took the bait, just as Hope wanted. "And what's that, Hope? You seem to have all the answers this evening."

Hope began to clear the table. She looked at Mazdon. "Well, of course, it's unconditional love."

Mazdon laughed. "There is no such thing, Hope. Where love is concerned, there are always rules."

Hope grinned. "Forever the romantic, aren't we?"

Mazdon burst into laughter. "Okay. I give. You win. I will agree with you."

"Good, the sooner you learn who is in charge here, the better for you," Hope stated matter-of-fact.

Mazdon grinned. "You're relentless. I now see why you are the assistant vice president of Spotlight Marketing Agency. You always get the last word in. Maybe that is why you are so successful with the campaigns."

Hope stopped. "Mazdon Elliott, you think I am successful. You're baiting me. Well, I won't jump. I agree with you one hundred percent. I must have the last word, because I am right about most things."

"Enough, Hope Sloan. Let's check on Faith and the puppies." She rose from the table at the same time Mazdon did. She lost her balance and fell into him with their plates and drinks. Sandwich, chips, and water covered Mazdon's shirt. Both began laughing. Mazdon could not resist. She was beautiful. He grabbed Hope and pulled her and all that she still had left in her hands towards his chest. "I've been wanting to do this since you walked into the office late and flustered that one day." Before she could remark that she was not *that* late, Mazdon leaned in and kissed her. It was not a quick kiss. It was a kiss that left her wanting to know more.

She pulled back and looked at him. Hope inhaled deeply. "Mazdon, are you okay?"

"I have never been more okay than this moment," Mazdon replied with a smile. He knew she was pondering what to do next. She was biting her lower lip. Without realizing it, he took his thumb and traced the outline of her lips with intense purpose. She parted her lips for Mazdon. This time, he took her top lip and nibbled and suckled, until it was swollen with desire. With ease, he placed his hand on her chin to pull her closer to his lips.

"Mazdon," Hope began. "We have to clean the puppies and place them back. Faith needs to rest before her next nursing. Remember, what Dr. Bayley told us. Every four hours."

Mazdon could not believe the moment was gone—or was it? He would help with the puppies, and then, he would resume where he left off: Hope's lips.

CHAPTER 21

All cleaned with baby wipes. All little bellies full. All sound asleep, and that included Faith. Hope needed to come up with names for them all. She would worry about that in the morning. Right now, her primary concern was "that" kiss and Mazdon. She stood up. He was looking at Hope. Hope knew if she returned the look or even a small gaze at him, she was going to melt. As funny as it sounded, it was true. That kiss just about did her in. She could not let Mazdon know the effect the kiss or he, himself, had. She needed to get him home and out of her thoughts.

"Mazdon, I just wanted to say thank you for all your help. To be honest, I was a bit worried about doing this all alone. You have done way more than you needed to, and for that, I can never repay you." She was continuing the conversation as she walked to the front door. "I know you must be worn out. I know I'll be fine. I understand if you need to go."

Mazdon began to laugh. He knew what Hope was doing. She was dismissing him, as if they were in a meeting at the office. She was good. Really good. He would play her game. He stood up and walked to where Hope stood by the door. She placed her hand on the door handle. He placed his hand on top of hers. "Thank you, Hope, for today. I am glad I was able to help. I will see you in a few days."

Almost there. He was almost through the door. Just a few more steps and she could breathe. Mazdon turned. He slid his arm around Hope's waist. He pulled her close. Mazdon reached for her. "Hope, are you sure you can handle Faith and the puppies all by yourself?"

Hope did not want him to know she did need help. She lied. "Lacie will be coming over later to stay with me. I'll be fine until then."

Mazdon smiled. She was trying to convince him. It was not working. "I don't believe you," Mazdon stated.

She could not pull away. There was security in his embrace. There was danger in being this close. Her body betrayed her. Hope was a strong, independent woman. She was career-driven. She was OCD and ADD. She was in control. SHE WAS WRAPPED IN THE ARMS OF HER BOSS!

Mazdon knew when her body language changed. He sensed the change. She looked up at him. Those eyes.

He could drown in those eyes. They were as blue as the ocean water and as bright as the morning sun. She had no idea the effect she was having on him. He lifted her lips to his. He nibbled until she parted them. He heard the intake of her breath. Mazdon's lips demanded more. Mazdon heard Hope groan in acceptance of his kiss. His hands moved to cup the side of her face. Hope had to steady herself by reaching for Mazdon's waist. She did not want to let go. The feeling of euphoria overcame Hope. She wanted to feel like this forever.

Mazdon stopped kissing Hope and pulled away. He looked down at her. She had placed her hands on his side. He did not want her to remove her hands. "Hope, do you want me to stop?"

Hope lost all sanity and, with one word, gave her answer. "No."

Mazdon closed the front door. He pushed Hope's body against the closed door. Before she could change her mind, Hope tippy-toed up to bring his lips back to where they belonged. She could not resist. It was as natural as a kiss of the feather floating down from heaven.

Mazdon's lips were everywhere. Mazdon grabbed her hips. She felt him nibble the side of her ear. She was breathless. Mazdon stepped back and like the breeze on the ocean, his hands had slid up her shirt. She inhaled. His thumb began a circular motion around her bellybutton. Hope was being tortured. Feelings she had never known she possessed were making it difficult to think straight.

She began to lift Mazdon's shirt over his head. She did not have to look at Mazdon. She knew he was well-built by just the way the shirt hugged his biceps and stretched across his skin. His chest was like a magnet to her hands. She felt Mazdon's heart beating beneath her fingers. She knew she was playing with fire. There was a moment that there would be no return.

Mazdon was unbuttoning her jeans. She felt the zipper slide down. He moved his hand inside to caress her. Hope was frozen. With strokes that were intent on finding her sweet spot, she shifted her legs. She arched her back. Mazdon held her with one arm. She was almost where he needed her. He wanted to take her to the pinnacle of ecstasy. Just a few more butterfly strokes. He could feel her becoming moist to his touch.

She was going to lose her balance. She was on a cloud, floating outside of her body, looking down at someone she did not recognize. She braced herself against Mazdon's muscular chest. She felt him. She knew what was going to happen next. The desire in her entire being was overwhelming. She could not stop it.

Mazdon looked at Hope. Her eyes were filled with desire and fire. Her body was opening for him to fulfill the need of completion. With every in and out stroke, his need rose to feel all of her. He needed to be inside of Hope. To have her hold him tight within the warmth and moistness of heaven. He slid her jeans down her legs. He helped her remove her legs until the jeans were thrown to the side. He placed his hand under her chin, so she would have to look at him.

Mazdon whispered, "Hope, I cannot promise you the future, but I can give you tonight. Tell me you want me as much as I want you."

Was this really happening? Was she getting ready to make love to her boss, Mazdon Elliott? No one would believe the chain of events that had taken place in bringing her to this point. She could not believe it. This was surreal. This was not real. He was not real. She looked at Mazdon. He was waiting for an answer. She could stop this. There was only one issue. She did not want this to stop.

Hope looked at Mazdon. "Yes, Mazdon, I want you."

Mazdon only heard the word "yes". Mazdon leaned Hope back, so he could kiss her into tomorrow. The feel of her soft lips against his was both infuriating and placating at the same time. It was not enough. Hope's lips betrayed her. She kissed him with every ounce of her being. When his warm lips met hers, the world stopped. She felt her feet leave the floor. She felt the heat of Mazdon's body against hers. He had picked her up. He remembered where her bedroom was from the morning's escapades. Mazdon felt Hope place her cheek against his bare chest. He stopped near the bed and gently placed her feet on the floor.

Hope's lips were swollen from Mazdon suckling on them. "Hope, open your eyes and look at me. I cannot promise you what tomorrow will hold, but I can tell you that I cannot leave you." Mazdon laid Hope back on her bed and lifted one arm over her head. He traced the silhouette of her body from the top to the underneath of her arm and then moved to the side of her breast. Hope arched her back. Mazdon's hand moved down to the curve of her waist. His hand moved behind to cup her backside. As he moved lower, his lips and tongue followed the journey.

Mazdon could not stop himself. He began to kiss her breast. Hope moaned. Oh, my lawd, his tongue was relentless. Swirling motions with his tongue around the nipple had placed Hope at his mercy. When Hope thought this was all she could handle, Mazdon slid his hand slowly between her legs.

"Hope, open yourself to me. Let me feel you." How much more could she withhold? Hope needed Mazdon inside of her. She needed a release. Her legs, without her awareness, parted and accepted the tip of Mazdon's manhood. Mazdon could not help himself. In and out, with teasing strokes. Heaven was for real. He had found it in Hope.

Hope reached for Mazdon's hips. She pulled him close. Mazdon took Hope's hands and guided them to his swollen manhood. He directed her to glide her hands up and down. Without hesitation, Mazdon entered Hope. She was warm and tight. Hope moaned.

Mazdon whispered to Hope, "I need to feel you, Hope. Wrap your legs around me." Mazdon braced himself with his hands on each side of Hope. He looked down at Hope. Her eyes closed. Her lips parted with satisfaction. "Open your eyes, Hope. I want to see you when I bring you to release." Hope opened her eyes. She watched as Mazdon lips drew closer to hers. He grabbed her hips, kissing her hard and leaving her breathless. Hope responded by moving in and out with

Mazdon's manhood. Each of their movements became as one. There was no separation. Their bodies were pressed together. No beginning. No end. Mazdon gave one thrust and Hope met him. She felt Mazdon lay his head against her shoulder. He kissed the side of her neck and rolled onto his back. Mazdon reached for her hand. "Hope," Mazdon began, I never meant…."

He looked over. She was asleep. As he turned, she rolled into Mazdon's side and had now placed her hand on his chest. He watched Hope as she slept. He kissed the top of her forehead and closed his eyes. He and Hope would need to talk in the morning. There were questions that needed to be asked and answered. For now, he would hold the beautiful woman in his arms with no thought of worry. Tonight had been perfect.

CHAPTER 22

Hope was dreaming. She could not wake up. The covers were wrapped around her as if she were a butterfly in the cocoon. She did not want to leave the comforts of her bed, but she knew the puppies would need to be nursed. She stretched her arms wide, and then, it hit her. She did not have any clothes on. Her hand leaned across the bed. There was no one there, but she knew HE had been. The indentation of the pillow confirmed that 100 percent. She did not see any trace of him. Mazdon Elliott had vanished into thin air.

She got up and put her sweats and tee on. As she was leaning down to put her footies on, that's when the realization of what had taken place a mere 24 hours ago dropped liked a bombshell. She walked into the kitchen area. Faith was nursing the puppies. She looked at Faith's water and food dishes. The food had been scattered a bit on the floor, which meant that Faith had, indeed, eaten. There were not just drops of water on the floor, but puddles. Hope smiled. This was how it was to be for the next eight weeks. At least with Faith, this was how the routine would be. She could not imagine that she would be making love to her boss, Mazdon Elliott, again. There was no chance of this. Hope could not let her guard down again.

Hope had relationships before Mazdon. Nothing serious. Her career came first. She knew what she wanted. It was to be independent and successful. She had never thought about being alone. She had Lacie. Lacie was her dearest friend. There was no one she trusted more. Hope glanced around the room. There was no sign that he had even walked through her doors. Where was he? Where did he go? Better yet, why did he not wake her to tell her he was leaving?

Hope needed some cold water. She needed that one drink that when you take it, it's as if the water is running through your veins and you can feel it. It brings a chill to your body. She opened the refrigerator door. As she was turning to reach for a glass, she saw the note. It had been placed to the side of the toaster. It read, "Open me first thing in the morning." Her hands began to shake. She did not want to open the envelope. She did not need to know what was inside. She sat down at the kitchen table, while keeping an eye on Faith and the puppies nursing. They would need to be cleaned, as well as Faith, before the next feeding. The envelope would wait.

Hope got up. The wipes had been left on the kitchen counter. She grabbed them and began the task of cleaning the puppies and then Faith. Once all the puppies were cleaned and placed back in the tub with blankets and Faith was resting, Hope returned to the table to where *that* envelope lay.

She reached for it. Before her fingers touched the envelope, her cell phone rang. Hope looked at the number. It was Lacie. This could only mean something had taken place at work. The current time was now after 9 a.m. "Good morning, Lace"—that's the nickname Hope had given Lacie—"how is the morning? How are you doing? Anything you need help with?" Hope knew these were loaded questions, but she did not want to share with Lacie the events of the evening nor of the morning.

Lacie began with, "I don't know what happened with Mazdon yesterday, but he's in a mood. He went straight to his office this morning, and he has yet to emerge. No one wants to confront him about any decisions regarding the campaigns. Any ideas why he may be pensive or stressed? Any ideas at all, Hope?"

She did not want Lacie to know what had transpired. Not yet anyways. And so, she did what she thought best. She lied to her best friend. "No, Lacie, I don't. I've been so busy contacting HR and scheduling vacation because of Faith and the birth of the puppies, I've not had time to take a breath. I'm sure whatever it is with Mazdon, it will pass by afternoon."

Lacie stated, "I sure hope so. We have another potential client interviewing us today, and you will not be here to smooth anything over, should it go awry."

Hope chuckled. "I'm not that big of a deal, but I appreciate your confidence in me. I've scheduled vacation for the next two to three weeks, until I can find a sitter for Faith and the puppies. I'll return to work then. If you want, swing over after work, and I'll introduce you to the family." Lacie commented she would love to and that she had to run. The morning meeting was about to be conducted, and Lacie needed to finalize materials before walking into the meeting. Hope told her she understood.

It was still there. In the same spot. In the same place. Unopened. What was the old saying "curiosity killed the cat?" Prayerfully, Hope had eight more lives. She opened the envelope with a butter knife from her kitchen drawer. Hope began to read and then she stopped. The first sentence started with:

"Dear Hope: What occurred last night CANNOT happen again. Emotions and the situation overwhelmed us. Please accept my apologies. Mazdon Elliott"

Three sentences. That was all. After what happened, she only deserved three sentences. She had never been written a letter like this – just writing her off. Who was he, and was he truly thinking that she would ever allow something like this to happen again? He was so arrogant and full of himself. Hope rose and grabbed her phone. She dialed the office.

The receptionist, Andee, answered. "Good morning, Spotlight Marketing Agency, how can I assist you today?" Hope asked her for the voicemail of Mazdon Elliott. Andee told Hope that Mr. Elliott was, indeed, in the office today, and she could transfer the call for her to speak directly to him. Hope thanked her, but said that would not be necessary—all she needed was his voicemail.

CHAPTER 23

Mazdon did not want to wake her. He did not know if he would be able to discuss with her what happened last night or not. He only knew it could not happen again. He placed his feet on the floor as quietly as possible. But before doing so, he had to scope out where his clothing had been thrown. His clothes were carelessly laying all about the bedroom. It was going to take all day to find them. He did, though.

After dressing, he did the only thing he could. He knew that Faith needed to be fed and the puppies needed nursing. It was early. Earlier than what he thought. He walked barefooted into the den, carrying his socks and shoes in one hand. He let Faith out the back through the kitchen door and watched as she did her morning business. He remembered where the dog food was and poured a half cup into Faith's bowl. The puppies were beginning to stir. If he didn't get Faith fed within the next ten minutes, Mazdon knew the entire neighborhood and Hope would be awake from the whining of the puppies. Faith came in without coaxing and went straight for her breakfast. The intuition that she had more important tasks to handle kept her focused on finishing her dog food. Mazdon wiped her face and cleaned her paws. Faith laid down to rest. This was the cue for Mazdon to pull the puppies out and have them latch on to Faith.

Putting on his socks and shoes, Mazdon counted them. Four beautiful bulldog puppies. All nursing. All were where they needed to be, except for him. If he did not leave now, he would be late for work and for the preparation of the presentation to a potential client. So, he did the next best thing. He wrote a note to Hope. He could only pray that she understood why he wrote what he did. Mazdon laid the note by the toaster and took one last look on Faith and the puppies and walked to the door. Leaving and locking the door behind him, he knew she was not going to be happy.

Pulling into his parking spot, Mazdon recognized that most of the staff had arrived. There were meetings this week of great importance that would open doors of opportunity for the agency into new areas. Mazdon needed the team to be on their toes. Walking in, he would be missing one of the most vital members of the team. He had left this particular team member at home snuggled under the blankets. He was prayerful that Lacie would lead the team this morning.

Mazdon stopped in his office before heading to Lacie's to confirm that all was set for the day. He picked his cell up and dialed her number. It rang and rang. He could not leave a voicemail; he needed to hear her. One more time, Mazdon thought to himself. If no answer, I'll call when I'm through with the conference. Again with the no mailbox set up. Lawd!!! Where was she? He hated he could not speak with her before going into the meeting. He would have to deal with Hope later.

CHAPTER 24

Hope did not know what she should expect. She had hoped that Mazdon would have returned her voicemail. There was only one flaw to that notion. She had told him to never speak to her, ever again. It was quite a straight-to-the-point voicemail she had left him. It started with "Mr. Elliott, this is Ms. Sloan. I found the note. There's no need to return this call. I completely understand." She hoped he could comprehend that she never wanted to have anything to do with him.

She heard Faith rustling around. It was time to nurse. She had cleaned all the babies and picked up all the pee pads where their business had been done. She needed to take a quick shower and then eat lunch. She was a bit hungry. She placed the puppies and watch as they latched on. This would give her about twenty minutes. She looked back one more time. Faith looked at her as if to say "make it snappy". Hope laughed. "I'm hurrying. I won't leave you like some other folk." She hoped that he could not find any documents for his meetings today. It would serve him right.

The shower was what she needed. She walked to the den where Faith was laying.

The puppies were snoring. She picked each up and placed them in the makeshift bed. She made sure all four were covered and cuddled against each other. The stuffed animals had been placed in the corners of the bin for playtime. The vet had told her that the stuffed animals would help strengthen the puppies' legs because they would have to climb over them to roam around. Hope cleaned Faith and fixed a quick lunch. She knew she was putting off the inevitable. She needed to call Lacie to be sure her clients and the campaigns were on target with timeframes and postings.

She dialed the number. Maybe Lacie was still in a meeting. Maybe she could leave a voicemail message. Maybe was not going to happen.

"I wondered if you were still alive. What took you so long to call? Is everything okay?" Lacie inquired.

Hope laughed. "I'm okay. You will never believe me in a thousand years. Are you sitting down?"

Lacie knew there were very few "sit down" talks that Hope conducted. It must be serious. Hope began with the emergency birth of Faith. Then Faith and the puppies needing to stay overnight. And, of course, bringing all home and getting adjusted to a routine. Hope left out the in-between. Right now, she did not want to share what had taken place between her and Mazdon. Lacie listened as Hope explained the last seventy-two hours.

"Well, it's been eventful. Is everyone okay? And when I say everyone, I am not talking about Faith and the puppies. I'm talking about you." Lacie stated. Hope could never lie to Lacie. She did not know how or why, but Lacie had that sixth sense.

Before Hope could stop them, a tear formed and then another. Lacie heard her. "You better spill the beans. Don't make me come over there. Or better yet, go to our boss, Mazdon Elliott, and inquire as to what happened."

Hope inhaled a breath. "It will be okay. I have taken four weeks of furternity leave." Lacie giggled. "Furternity leave? I can't wait to hear this."

Hope smiled. "Well, it's just like maternity leave, except my baby is more than one and has four beautiful paws. So just like all mommas need to be with their child, I, too, need to be with Faith and the puppies. So, therefore, I need time off for furternity leave."

Hope began with what she really wanted to know. "How is today going? How is the Hounds Up Tails Down pitch campaign? Did they accept?" Lacie told her that Mazdon seemed a bit preoccupied this morning when he arrived. In the meeting, there a few times he seemed disinterested but the team made sure that the agency pulled through. Hounds Up Tails Down was happy to begin the relationship with the Agency. They loved the direction that the agency was ready to take them. Hounds Up Tails Down was to get back within forty-eight hours of any changes and then, the documents would be signed. "Did he say anything about me?" Hope asked.

"No, not a peep," Lacie commented. Hope could hear chatting in the background. Lacie had work to do. She would call Lacie later when they could talk. As she hung the phone up, her first thought was, *He didn't even say a word.*

Mazdon had no idea what came over him. The team did not comment on his inattentiveness this morning. This was so unlike him. He was always in control. He knew they noticed, because he noticed. And he knew why the morning had not gone as planned. All he could think about was her. What was she doing? How was Faith? Was she keeping the routine going with nursing the puppies? Had she thought about him and the night they spent together? Questions that had no answers. And, unless he called or went back to her home, he would never know.

As the day wore down with calls, meetings, follow up, and the finalization of the documents needed for the new client, Hounds Up Tails Down, Mazdon hated to admit, he was tired. He did not want to speak to anyone else. He wanted to go home, shower, and chill for the remainder of the night. He grabbed his briefcase and threw whatever notes he would need as a "just in case" study tonight. Walking down the hallway, he overheard Lacie, "I'll call you when I get home and give you all the details of the happenings of the day and meetings." There was only one person who needed the details of the day, and that was somebody that was not in attendance. She would be calling Hope. Maybe he should call Hope as a courtesy and fill her in on the day. After all, she was the team lead.

Mazdon buckled up and started his car. He needed to call before he left the parking lot. He did not want to be driving and trying to concentrate on Hope and the conversation. He dialed her number. No answer. And, of course, he could not leave a voicemail. He recalled her telling him that, specifically. Lawd, this woman was doing everything she could to aggravate him. And yet, she had done nothing. So, why was he so upset? He did not want to admit it to himself. He was worried about Hope. He was beginning to care about Hope. This could not happen. He would not allow it to happen.

CHAPTER 25

Faith and the puppies had just finished nursing. She saw the cell phone vibrate on the kitchen counter. She knew Lacie would be calling to inform her of the day's activities. She rose to go pick it up. As she looked down at the number, it was *not* Lacie. It was HIM. No way on the moon was she going to answer. He could bite the cheeks of her hiney for all she cared. Actually, he could fall off the face of the earth, and it would not matter to her. She knew he could not leave a voicemail, because she had never set it up - for this exact reason – unwanted callers wanting to leave unwanted messages. She laughed. Serves him right.

Lacie headed out and saw Mazdon in his car. He was on the phone. Oh wait, he was not on the phone. That was a quick call. She wanted to be sure that he was happy with all that transpired with the meetings today. But the look on his face was a sure sign he did not want to be bothered. Tomorrow, she would speak with him. She needed to call Hope and fill her in. She hated to use the phone while driving, even if on hands-free and using speaker. She got in the car and dialed

Hope's number. "Hey there, what took you so long?" Of course, she would ask that, Lacie laughed. Always eager to get things out of the way and clear them from her agenda. Yep, that was Hope, and that was the reason why she was such a great lead for their team. She was hands-on and finished what she committed to doing.

"The day was profitable. Two new clients signed. We begin the videos and marketing layout tomorrow. It was a pretty smooth day," Lacie told her. Lacie could tell that was not what she wanted to hear. "Instead of beating around the bush, just ask me, Hope."

"How was Mazdon?" Lacie could tell that Hope was sincere when asking.

"He was okay. He was a bit preoccupied. His mind was not in the right place. Not on his A game. But we finished the day strong. Is there anything you want to tell me? Do you know the reason why he was not the typical Mazdon Elliott?"

Hope began with, "Lacie, I don't know how or what to say. So, I'll just say it. We made love last night." Lacie dropped the phone in the floorboard. She did not know whether she heard Hope correctly. As she was shuffling for the phone, she could hear Hope in the background. "Lacie, are you still there. Did you hear what I said?"

Lacie returned the question with hysteria. "Are you freaking kidding me? You did what? And the what, you did with our boss?"

Hope cleared her throat. "Calm down, you heard me. It was a mistake. I know that, and so does he. It will not happen again."

Lacie inhaled. "How and when and why did this happen?"

Hope laughed. "Just like it always does when two people are attracted to each other. It just happened. I cannot turn back time. I need to focus on Faith and the puppies and finding good homes for the puppies. I am fine. He will be fine. I need to keep my job. If you can do a daily briefing with me, I know I can still be a huge contributor and still keep my job. Is this possible?"

Lacie sarcastically stated, "You throw *all* this on me and ask me if we can do a daily briefing? I'm still wrapping my head around the fact *you* made love with *him*. But by all means, Hope, sure we can. Daily briefing. Details and agenda shared. I'm there for you."

Hope told Lacie to calm down and breathe. "It will work out. Trust me."

They spoke a bit more, and then, both agreed that 2 p.m. would be their set time to discuss the day's going ons. This would allow Hope to take care of Faith and nursing the puppies in the morning. She would then be able to log in to the office network and review client files and get up to speed on the existing clients, as well as the new clients. Lacie informed Hope that if she needed to talk, she was there for her friend. Just knowing this, Hope knew she could make these next four weeks work.

CHAPTER 26

Four weeks. Had it been four weeks since they had last spoken, since they had last seen each other, since they had made love? Twenty-eight days, six hundred seventy-two hours, forty thousand three hundred twenty minutes, or two million four hundred nineteen thousand two hundred seconds – BUT WHO WAS COUNTING? *Certainly, not me*, Mazdon thought to himself as he pushed the calculator back inside the desk. Enough. She was due back today. She would have to see him. He did not think it possible, but she had worked from home and had done an exceptional job. The team stayed in flow with all deadlines. When ZOOM meetings were scheduled, she was not on there, but followed up via email with her notations and concerns. He needed to tell her what he had discovered.

There was an office meeting this morning. Her first one since being on furternity leave. It was inevitable. She was going to see him. She needed to be strong. No reaction needed to be revealed. She had made a decision that after the puppies had been placed, she would be looking for another job. She had done the research while off, and knew there were other positions available. She did not want to leave, but the circumstances left her no other alternative. She had missed him. She could not work with him and not think about what had transpired between them. Her mind told her to be logical. Her heart told her something different. She needed to tell him what she had discovered.

The meeting was starting. She assumed her position in the very back, like always. He had not yet entered. The team had welcomed her back. All were dying to know how Faith and the puppies were. Lacie had handed out the agenda for today to everyone. It was going to be busy. She heard his footsteps. She knew the exact moment he touched the door handle. He walked in and looked around, as if he were counting attendance. The meeting began on time. Nothing out of the norm. Everyone began to scoot their chairs back, ready to exit the conference room and tackle the day. One by one, Mazdon thanked them as they left. It was just her and Lacie in the room.

Hope looked at Lacie and reached for her hand. "Stay with me."

Lacie smiled. "Like he's going to allow that. Scream if you need me."

Hope gritted her teeth at Lacie. "Not funny, Lacie." Lacie squeezed her hand for reassurance and walked out the door.

Both stood there. Both not making a move. Hope looked down at the papers she held in her hand. Her thoughts were racing. *Please don't let him come over here.* And then, he walked towards her. Of course, he was walking towards her. He stopped. He reached for the papers and removed them from Hope's hands. She had nothing to hold on to. He raised her chin with his fingers. "Look at me, Hope."

Hope had no idea what overcame her, but her fingers had a mind of their own. "What do you mean, look at you?" She pointed her finger at him. "Why did you leave that note? Nothing for four weeks. No phone calls. Nothing."

Mazdon grabbed her finger and intertwined his with hers. "You know I called. You chose to ignore my calls. You have caller ID. And, unfortunately, I have no way of leaving a voicemail. So, your turn. Why didn't you return my calls?"

Hope was speechless. She had not made an attempt to return his calls. "It's just as much my fault as yours. Fine, I admit it."

His touch sent an intensity of warmth through Hope. This could not be happening. Mazdon pulled her into his arms. She did not resist. She could not resist. She had missed his strength. Hope had missed him, her boss, but more her friend. Mazdon leaned in to kiss her. Lawd, with her emotions running on overload, he prayed she would not pull away. It was there as he knew. The chemistry, the spark of electricity, the heat of passion. He knew she felt it by the way her lips opened for him. Hope moaned in satisfaction. It was a dream. This was not real.

"Hope, I know you are going to think me crazy for what I am about to say. But I know what I know. Until that night, I did not know I could feel this way. I thought my career would always come first. I was wrong. You have opened my heart to a journey I never thought I would take. Actually, it's plain and simple. I'm falling in head over paws in love you." Hope looked at Mazdon and traced his lips. She heard the word paws and love. A great combination, if she did say so herself.

"Mazdon, I don't know what tomorrow will bring, but I know that I want you in all of my tomorrows." Mazdon grinned. He kissed her hard. He kissed her longingly. This was the beginning of hope, faith, and love – isn't that what is always needed in any relationship?

SIX MONTHS LATER

The church was exquisite. It was decorated in magenta, black, and white along the pews, with petals scattered on the outside of the runner. Candles were lit on the steps where they would kneel to take their vows. He stood there, waiting and watching. In these last six months, the team had grown tighter in the agency with Hope's guidance. Clientele and revenue had increased. He remembered the words she had used, "We are blessed." He did not think about what it had meant when she said it and now, he knew.

It was not a large wedding. It was small and personable, as Hope had desired. He wanted her to be happy. Faith was sitting so obediently by Mazdon's legs. She was dressed in the hottest of pink rhinestone leashes. The music began, and his face looked towards the doors that were opening. He saw her. Hope would be his. Their relationship had grown from friends to more than just. Isn't that what love should be .... more than just? Her parents walked Hope down the aisle. They placed Hope's hand in Mazdon's.

He whispered so only Hope could hear, "I'll love you forever and a day. Are you ready?"

Hope looked at Mazdon. Then, she looked at Faith. "I choose Faith. I choose you, Mazdon Elliott. Without pause, without doubt, I choose to love you. Yes, I am ready."

"And now, these three remain – faith, hope, and love. But the greatest of these is love." 1st Corinthians 13:13

KENTUCKY ROMANCE AUTHOR

The Day You Go from Romance Junkie to # 1 Best-
Selling Kentucky Romance Author

de de began pursuing her dream of becoming a romance author at the age of 30. Born and raised on a farm in Rooster Run, Kentucky, de de was raised on the core values of the 3Cs (kindness, caring and compassion). Throughout her young adulthood, de de volunteered in the community with her family, and specifically, her grandmother, Bea. Growing up in the country, romance novels were her escape to another world. de de knew that one day, her dream of writing a romance novel would come true. Fast forward to 2018, when de de picked the book back up that she had begun in her early 30s. As in life, circumstances and direction change the course, BUT never the ending goal. Learning the industry and working with her publisher, Beyond Publishing, God opened many doors and many connections, and de de has never looked back.

de de became a published Kentucky romance author in 2018. She is the #1 best-selling Kentucky romance author of the Two Degrees Series, which features her son, Bo, as the male model. Little did de de know that her child would become the next "FabiBo".

de de is working on her new series – RESCUE ME (animals and love), which will debut in 2021. The story of rescue, the story of love, the story of FURever. The first book title is "FURternity Leave – When All You Need Is Faith".

de de has served as a board member of The Dream Factory of Louisville, Kentucky, Opal's Dream Foundation, Spalding University – Athletic Board, as well as volunteered with other charitable entities. de de received the coveted 2018 Spirit of Louisville Foundation - WLKY Bell Award for her volunteerism within her community and now serves on the board as trustee.

de de is active within the pageant industry. She is the co-preliminary director of the Miss My Old

Kentucky Home (a prelim to the state /national of the Miss America system). In addition, she is the co-director of the Miss Hillview, Miss Buttermilk, and Miss Bullitt Blast Festival prelims (Kentucky State Festival).

FAMILY (family always mean I love you), and this is true in de de's life. So many kind-hearted folk have travelled the journey. She has been married for over 35 years to her best friend (Scott) from high school. She has two sons and two rescued fur babies.

de de encourages others to live by HIS word – Acts 20:35.

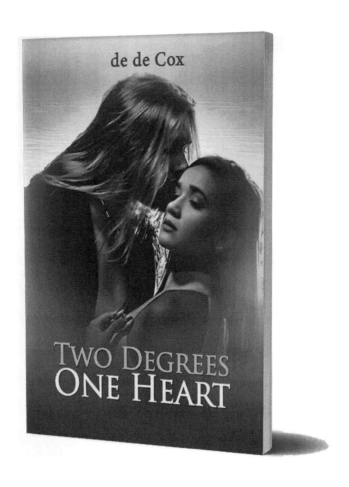

de de Cox

TWO DEGREES
ONE HEART

It was going to be one of those Monday mornings. As Logan was jogging into the hospital entrance, he could see several others were in his dilemma. Running a bit behind. It was Logan's first day of his new travel assignment. He did not want to be late. Logan knew the first impression was the lasting impression.

Winter knew she could not turn away. This was the man she was in love with. This was the man she wanted to spend the rest of her life with.

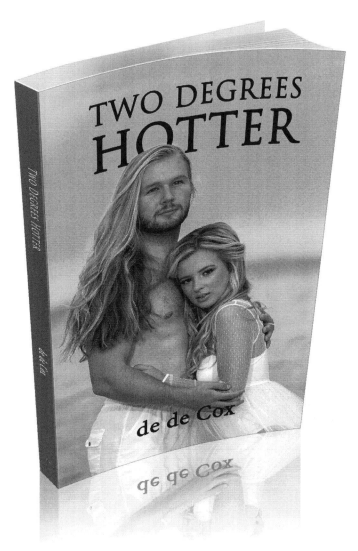

"Two Degrees Hotter brings to life not just the story of love but the struggle that can accompany the every day journey. When something is so precious, it is worth the effort. There is a point of the understanding that in our lives there is always a moment somewhere in time that a connection is or has been made. True love is a never ending connection.

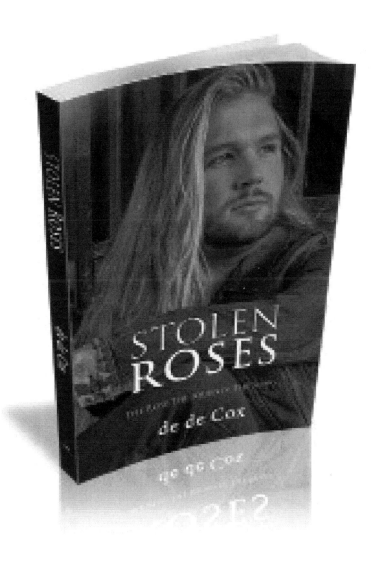

There could be no doubt. She read it multiple times. The note had said it all and yet, it said nothing. Never did she think that her heart could feel pain such as this. Plans had been made. He was her rock. He had been there since she was five. Growing up and sharing dreams, hopes, and goals had become their special time together.

The story of rescue...
the story of love...
the story of
FURever

ALL HIS LOVE FOR
Christmas

de de Cox

She shook her head at them. They had stopped. They would not move. The whining and barking were incessant. What in the world was going on? Why was it taking so long? As she walked towards the three, an uneasy feeling came over her. She drew closer to the edge of the road. Dr. Harper True, knew something or someone was down below. She could only pray that whoever or whatever was alive. As she slid down the embankment, her worse fears were coming true. It was not something. It was someone.